"I don't believe you…"

"Don't believe me about what?"

Rafe eased closer, a glint of determination in his eyes. "Why you said you bid on me."

Gina felt herself rise to the challenge. "Oh, yeah? Why do you think I bid on your cowboy experience?"

"Because you wanted it."

"Aren't you full of yourself."

"I didn't say you wanted me." But his heated gaze moved to her lips.

She wasn't about to admit anything. "You're saying I wanted a horseback ride?"

"Admit it, Gina. You wanted to experience *this* cowboy."

His deep tone and sensual words vibrated through her, bringing desire and passion to life.

"Good news," he said, brushing his hand against hers.

She shivered in reaction, barely getting the words out. "What news?"

"*There's a second…*

Bidding on a Tex…   the Texas Cattlem…

Dear Reader,

I was excited to participate in the Texas Cattleman's Club series! It's such fun to collaborate with my fellow Desire authors.

It's been a while since I wrote a cowboy story, and I remembered how much I enjoyed those rugged, rustic heroes, especially one who's forced out of his comfort zone!

In *Bidding on a Texan*, rancher Rafe Cortez-Williams navigates his own course, different from his father's and brothers'. His path is complicated by the gorgeous and sexy but seemingly spoiled Gina Edmond, who forces him to expand his horizons and question his preconceptions.

I hope you enjoy the story!

Barbara

BARBARA DUNLOP

—

BIDDING ON A TEXAN

Special thanks and acknowledgment are given to Barbara Dunlop for her contribution to the Texas Cattleman's Club: Heir Apparent miniseries.

HARLEQUIN®
DESIRE™

Recycling programs for this product may not exist in your area.

ISBN-13: 978-1-335-73517-1

Bidding on a Texan

Harlequin Enterprises ULC
22 Adelaide St. West, 40th Floor
Toronto, Ontario M5H 4E3, Canada
www.Harlequin.com

Printed in U.S.A.

New York Times and *USA TODAY* bestselling author **Barbara Dunlop** has written more than forty novels for Harlequin, including the acclaimed Chicago Sons series for Harlequin Desire. Her sexy, lighthearted stories regularly hit bestseller lists. Barbara is a three-time finalist for the Romance Writers of America's RITA® Award.

Books by Barbara Dunlop

Harlequin Desire

Chicago Sons

Sex, Lies and the CEO
Seduced by the CEO
A Bargain with the Boss
His Stolen Bride

Gambling Men

The Twin Switch
The Dating Dare

Texas Cattleman's Club: Heir Apparent

Bidding on a Texan

Visit her Author Profile page at Harlequin.com, or barbaradunlop.com, for more titles.

You can also find Barbara Dunlop on Facebook, along with other Harlequin Desire authors, at Facebook.com/harlequindesireauthors!

For Mom and Dad,
who packed up four kids to vacation
on a cattle ranch.

One

Rafe Cortez-Williams opened RCW Steakhouse in Royal, Texas, against his father's wishes. He was expected to carry on the family legacy, running the cattle ranch that had been in Mustang County for multiple generations. But Rafe had four brothers, all of them highly skilled cowboys, and the ranch felt crowded at times.

So three years ago he made the break.

His brick-fronted steakhouse in the heart of downtown was a local hit from the start. It served tender steaks and juicy burgers charred to perfection along with seafood sides and a few Asian fusion specialties. RCW was considered a prime venue for celebrations and special events, which meant patrons were open to higher-priced indulgences.

Despite his father's doubts, things had worked out exceptionally well for Rafe—at least they had up to now.

"Decent lunch crowd today?" RCW head chef JJ Yeoh was working at the long gas stove top in the center of the big kitchen. He spoke over the sizzle of steaks and sautéing vegetables, and the clatter of pans and dishes as the kitchen staff efficiently prepared dozens of meals.

"We're completely full out there," Rafe replied, swiftly stepping to one side as a waitress passed by carrying two sizzling T-bones with all the trimmings. "I don't think the brand's been tainted…at least not yet."

"None of the scandal is on you," JJ said. He glanced up from where he was spicing a skillet of shrimp. "All you did was invest in a good cause—generously."

"Our name was strongly attached to Soiree on the Bay. There'll be blowback. Don't you doubt it."

JJ, always an optimist, gave a shrug. "People still like to eat."

"People can eat at other places."

"Ahhh, but not like they can eat here." The chef turned his attention back to his cooking, stirring the mixture in the hot skillet, releasing a spicy aroma that made Rafe's stomach growl.

JJ was right about that. But in the end, it might not matter.

Because if Rafe couldn't pay the second mortgage, not even his top chef's signature sambal shrimp dish was going to save him. But he didn't have the heart to tell JJ about the company's true financial peril.

The noise level ebbed and flowed as waitstaff came and went with meals and baskets of homemade sourdough bread. A busboy entered through the far door to deposit a load of dishes with the washing staff. On a busy day like this, it was important to get the tables bused quickly and set up for the next party. Rafe hated to leave people waiting in the foyer.

"I'm going to take a walk around. See you in a bit."

JJ gave a nod, most of his focus on his cooking as he started on the next order.

Rafe like to do a circuit of the dining room every half hour or so. He wasn't the kind of owner who intruded on the customers' dining experience. He liked to think he had an innate sense of who wanted a hello, who coveted a brief chat and who wanted to be left alone to enjoy the company at their own table. The clues were in people's expressions and their body language, but mostly in their eye contact.

He was particularly cautious with couples. The last thing he wanted to do was interrupt a romantic evening for two. Those were sacrosanct. Not that he'd had one himself in the past while.

Rafe made his way down the short kitchen hallway and into the main dining room. His restaurant was set up in three separate sections, and the sections were further divided by strategically placed wooden pillars and narrow, glass-fronted carved wood cabinets. The layout cut down on the ambient noise and gave diners additional privacy.

He checked the front dining room first with its muted lighting, rich wood panels and open wine racks.

He approached a party of six. It looked like a multi-generational group, and he guessed the older man at the head of the table was the host.

"Good afternoon," he said, taking in the whole table. "I'm Rafe Cortez-Williams, owner of the RCW. How are you enjoying your meals?"

The party looked to be about halfway through dining.

"Delicious," the older man said with a grin, gesturing to his plate that held a thick rib eye steak. "What's the secret to your baked potato?"

"A touch of cayenne," Rafe answered. "Gives it a little zing."

"I liked that little zing," the man responded.

Rafe looked around at the other diners to see if they had anything to say.

A pretty blonde woman who looked to be in her twenties lifted her blown crystal goblet and gave it a rock. "These are deliciously dangerous," she said.

"Is that the guava cranberry or the raspberry?" Rafe asked.

"Guava cranberry."

"That's one of my favorites," he said. "Would you like another?" As he asked the question, he discreetly signaled behind his back for the waitress.

The blonde woman looked to the man sitting next to her.

"Go for it." The man answered the question in her eyes with good humor. "I'm driving."

"It's a family reunion," a woman to the right of the older man said.

Rafe assumed she was his wife.

Their waitress, Shirley, arrived by Rafe's side.

"I believe this woman might like another guava cranberry blend," he stated, raising his brow at the woman in a question.

"Yes, please," she laughed.

"Enjoy your meal and the rest of the reunion," he said to them all, leaving them in Shirley's hands.

Smiling to himself, he moved on, stopping at a few

more tables before he entered the southern dining room at the back of the restaurant.

Rafe swiftly scanned the vicinity from the doorway, barely believing what he was seeing. Gina Edmond, the only daughter of oil magnate Rusty Edmond, had graced RCW *in person*.

Though Rafe had never met Gina, he knew the gorgeous and glamorous heiress on sight. She was Royal's most pampered princess, and RCW was definitely not her usual haunt.

It hit Rafe then why she was here. She couldn't exactly show her face at the Texas Cattleman's Club right now. Not after that colossal scandal that had rocked the town.

At the center of that scandal was Billy Holmes, the man who was at the very least a close friend of the Edmonds, and possibly Gina's secret half-brother. Billy had disappeared with millions of dollars of investment in the Soiree on the Bay festival. And by all accounts, the Edmond houseguest had not only doomed the festival to failure but was directly responsible for bringing some of the local businesses to bankruptcy.

The last person Rafe wanted to chat with was Gina Edmond and…his attention moved to her dining companion. It was Sarabeth, Gina's estranged mother. Well, not so estranged anymore since Sarabeth had returned to Royal and was planning her wedding, a very *expensive* yacht-board wedding, proving the Edmonds weren't suffering in the slightest from the financial ruin of Soiree on the Bay.

A waitress slipped past Rafe, and he reminded himself to get on with business. Gina was here. She was a customer, and he'd be professional if it killed him.

* * *

Gina Edmond was aware she'd spent her whole life on the gilded social glide path that came with being Rusty Edmond's only daughter. Rusty was a legend in the Texas oil business, a prominent member of the Texas Cattleman's Club, and a mover and shaker in the Royal Chamber of Commerce. For twenty-six years, Gina had been treated with automatic respect and had enjoyed the advantages of her family's position.

But her glide path had come to an abrupt halt.

The family was no longer venerated by their fellow citizens and TCC members. Instead, the Edmonds were *all* treated with suspicion, even though they'd had nothing to do with Billy's crimes. Her family had been duped along with everyone else, and they'd suffered for it.

"After the false accusation about Asher..." her mother, Sarabeth, was saying from across the dining table. "And now Billy and the missing money on top of it all. You kids have way too much on your plates. I wonder if we should postpone the wedding."

"Don't you dare postpone!" Gina countered. Her stepbrother, Asher, had been exonerated of the embezzlement charge and was out of jail now.

Gina was looking forward to the wedding. She'd been estranged from her mother since she was eight years old. She'd been angry for most of those years, but she'd since learned about her mother's troubled past. And after getting to know her mother these past few months, the rift between them was healing. Sarabeth deserved her hard-won happiness with local rancher Brett Harston.

"It seems…" Sarabeth was clearly searching for the right word.

"It seems wonderful, exhilarating and inspirational," Gina finished for her. "It's just what the community needs to take their minds off the disaster. Everyone loves a happy ending."

"I feel selfish," Sarabeth admitted, looking unconvinced.

"You'd be selfish to cancel," Gina countered.

She wanted her mother to be happy, but she honestly believed the rest of her sales pitch as well. Royal needed a distraction, and the wedding would provide it for the four hundred guests on the invitation list, covering many of the TCC members and most of the families and businesses that had been hurt by the cancellation of Soiree on the Bay.

"You think so?" Sarabeth asked.

"I *know* so." Gina reached out to pat her mother's hand. "And if you're going to worry about anything," she joked, attempting to lighten the mood, "worry about me getting a date for the wedding."

Sarabeth waved away Gina's concern. "You can get all the dates you want and then some. Look at you!"

Gina knew her looks were fine. She wasn't exactly the life of the party, but she thought she had a decent sense of humor. And if her grades were anything to go by, she was reasonably intelligent. She'd earned a bachelor's degree in business administration from Texas Southern. Still, she'd never truly clicked with a boyfriend, and she already knew most of the men in Royal.

"You can't stick to such a strict list of attributes," Sarabeth said, taking a thoughtful sip of her chardonnay.

Gina leaned forward to lower her voice. "I don't have

a list of attributes." That said, she supposed she did have a few general criteria she'd look for in a man. Honesty, for starters, as well as someone who was honorable, funny, successful or, she supposed, more like happy in their chosen career. She wasn't a snob about money.

"Who would be perfect?" Sarabeth asked. "Toss out a name."

Gina didn't have a name.

Just then she caught sight of a tall, dark, broad-shouldered man in a finely cut jacket chatting with the diners at another table. His smile was bright white and beautiful. His dark eyes were warm and friendly. And judging by the laughter from the four people sitting at the table, he had a good sense of humor.

"What about him?" Gina asked, giving a discreet nod.

Her mother looked over her shoulder. She stared for a moment then turned back, a worried expression on her face. "Uh… Gina…"

"Shhh. He's coming over."

The man strode their way, looking self-assured and in his element. But as his gaze met hers his brown eyes hardened. His beautiful smile disappeared, and his jaw went taut.

"Ms. Edmond," he said, giving her a curt nod. "Mrs. Edmond," he said to Sarabeth.

"Hello," Gina murmured in return, puzzled by his attitude.

"I'm Rafe Cortez-Williams, owner of the RCW."

Recognition jolted Gina like a splash of ice water.

RCW was a major sponsor of Soiree on the Bay. Rafe had been among the biggest financial losers in the festival debacle. And he blamed her. Or at least he blamed her *family* for his loss.

"I hope you're having an enjoyable lunch." His friendly scripted words were at odds with his hostile demeanor.

"Everything is delicious," Sarabeth said in a perfectly amicable tone.

Gina shot her mother a look of confusion. Why was she kissing up to the guy?

"I'm very glad to hear that. Please, enjoy." And then he was gone, off to the next table where he smiled and treated them to the compelling glow in his gorgeous eyes.

"Unfortunately, not the guy for you," Sarabeth said.

"Why were you so nice?"

"Rafe lost a big chunk of money. He deserves to be angry."

"It wasn't *our* fault. It was Billy's fault…maybe." They didn't even know that much for sure.

"And if Billy's your half-brother?"

"We don't know he did it, and we don't know for sure he's Dad's son."

Sarabeth lifted her glass again, gazing contemplatively at the pale wine. "Remember, I was married to your father back then."

Gina took a drink of her merlot, needing it. She'd gotten past the squirming discomfort at discussing her father's infidelity with her mother, but it was far from her favorite subject. "Antoinette Holmes admits she also slept with other men."

"Maybe," Sarabeth said, looking unconvinced by that detail.

"Back to your wedding," Gina said, wanting to move

her thoughts past Billy and *well past* Rafe Cortez-Williams, since he was obviously *far* from her perfect man. "Let's talk about your hair…"

Sarabeth easily switched topics. "What do you think? Up or down?" She gathered her blond hair at the back of her neck and pulled it up to demonstrate.

As they delved into an in-depth discussion about hairdos, veils and age-appropriate wedding gowns, from the corner of her eye, Gina caught another glimpse of Rafe. She tried to ignore it, but he snagged her attention—his square shoulders, confident walk, that thick head of lustrous dark hair…

He might be all wrong for her, but he sure was smoking hot.

"Gina?" Sarabeth prompted her.

"Hmm?" She gave herself a little shake.

"I like the idea of tea-length. I don't want to dress up all frothy like some dewy-eyed ingenue."

"Do they even use that term anymore?"

Sarabeth chuckled. "Ingenues? Maybe not. But you know what I mean."

"We need to go talk to Natalie Valentine," Gina said, referring to the owner of a local bridal shop.

It might not be her own wedding, but she was excited about planning her mom's. Maybe someday it would be hers. Her thoughts went back to Rafe for a split second before she banished him. Sure, he'd look good in a tux at the front of church, but there was a whole lot more to a marriage than a guy who could rock the wedding.

"I *am* marrying a rancher," Sarabeth mused. "What about country rustic?"

"But you're marrying him on a yacht. Maybe go for a classic or elegant style?"

Sarabeth closed her eyes.

Gina couldn't seem to stop herself from glancing to the archway that led to the front dining room. Rafe was on the other side of it in the distance, and she gazed at him for a minute longer, thinking there was no law against looking.

"I'm thinking tea-length, slightly A-line," Sarabeth said, opening her eyes. "Ivory silk, maybe a thin organza overlay and flat lace on a sweetheart neckline with cap sleeves?"

"That's a very detailed picture."

"Can you see it?"

Gina *could* see it, and it was beautiful. She smiled. "Yes. Not too froufrou, but formal enough for the opulent surroundings."

"That's it!" her mother said, sitting back. "Next, we do you."

Sarabeth left to meet her fiancé, Brett, while Gina stayed behind to take care of the RCW tab. She hesitated over the tip amount. She wanted to be generous to their waitress, but she was afraid Rafe might see a large tip as flaunting the family wealth, especially in light of the collective losses of Royal businesses from Soiree on the Bay.

Then she laughed at her own foolishness, realizing Rafe would never even see the tip. What were the chances he went through a day's credit card receipts? Slim to none. She tipped big and punched in her PIN.

There. Done.

She came to her feet, smoothing the front of her sleeveless black-and-white dress and slipping her olive green handbag over her shoulder. She walked with confidence in her jungle-patterned pumps. The spike-heeled shoes weren't made for long walks, but they did great things for her calves, and they'd get her as far as her Jaguar convertible.

As she rounded a polished wood pillar near the front foyer, a man stepped unexpectedly out in front of her. She stumbled, nearly falling into his chest.

His hands came out, grasping her upper arms to steady her, and she looked up to find it was Rafe. Strong hands, handsome face, sinfully sexy lips...

Gina told her brain to shut up already.

"Sorry," he said, then obviously registered who she was. He let go of her like she was contagious, that frown reappearing on his face.

"My fault," she said, because it was, and she didn't have to like him to tell the truth. "I was in a hurry."

He glanced into the dining area behind her. "Your mother?"

"Left to meet with her fiancé."

"Ah, yes, Brett Harston."

"Right. You would know Brett."

"Ranching fraternity."

Rafe didn't look much like a rancher. His face was tanned a deep brown. His hands were broad and strong, but she hadn't felt thick calluses on his fingertips like most ranchers'.

She wondered how long it had been since he rode the range on his huge family ranch.

"I haven't seen you in here before now," Rafe drawled, his watchful gaze betraying his assumption. He'd concluded she was persona non grata at the TCC. He was right, but that didn't excuse his rudeness.

"Are you trying to start an argument?" she asked bluntly.

"No...yes...maybe." There was a hint of amusement in his expression along with what seemed like a flare of admiration for her grit.

She might have laughed at the comeback if he wasn't being such a jerk. "We were victims, too, you know. Just like everyone else."

His dark brows went up in obvious amazement. *"You?"*

"Yes, me."

"The Edmond princess, a victim of financial misfortune?" He made a show of peering out the front window to the parking lot. "Let me guess which car you're driving."

"Well, that's irrelevant."

He took his time looking over her designer outfit. "Where, exactly, are you going to have to cut back, Princess?"

Her clothes were expensive, sure. But, again, *irrelevant*. "Don't call me that."

"It fits." He waited a moment. "You don't have an answer, do you?"

"An answer for what? For you being so rude?"

"On where you're personally cutting back. Give me one concrete example of the festival embezzlement impacting your exclusive lifestyle, and I'll apologize unreservedly."

She didn't have a quick answer for that.

"That's none of your business," she huffed.

He laughed at that, a full, rich sound.

"Well, clearly nothing's changed around *here* yet,"

Gina pointed out, glancing around at the bustling staff and the upscale decor.

Rafe sobered. "You can't see what's happening under the surface."

"You can't see what's happening under my surface, either." The Edmonds might not be in an immediate cash crisis, but their reputation had been savaged, starting with Asher's arrest and then with Billy's disappearance. And the fallout from that was just beginning.

Never mind that she and her brothers felt honor bound to try to fix the mess. She'd never admit it to someone like Rafe, but she did feel some responsibility for the catastrophe since it was her family that brought Billy into the community.

Rafe considered her for a minute. Up close, her initial attraction to his looks, his powerful presence and his graceful movements grew even more potent. She felt hot and prickly with awareness of him as a man.

"You want to show me?" he asked, his low, deep voice reverberating around her.

She was taken aback by the question. It could be interpreted in a whole host of different ways, some of them extremely seductive. Her face and neck warmed with her reckless thoughts.

"Hang on," he said. "I didn't mean it that way…"

She didn't know what she hated more, that he seemed to be able to read her mind or that she seemed to be able to read his.

"I didn't think you did," she answered tartly, willing her hormones to calm the heck down.

"Then why the blush?"

"I don't blush."

"You're blushing now." He was making it worse.

"I'm *angry* now," she said.

"Why?"

She didn't have a quick answer for that either, but she tried her best. "Because…because, you're being so rude!"

"Me?" He feigned surprise.

"Yes, you."

"I only asked about the more subtle impacts of the embezzlement situation on your family."

She narrowed her eyes, not buying his innocent act for a moment. "Yeah, right."

He shook his head pityingly. "Oh, Gina. You're so used to men falling at your feet in abject adoration that you don't recognize anything else."

She wasn't. She didn't. She hadn't just done that… Had she?

Two

Rafe was nothing more than an ordinary guy.

Sadly, that meant he was cursed like all the rest with an undeniable urge to fall at Gina Edmond's feet in abject adoration. But he'd never do it. He was far too smart for that. But he wasn't immune to the unmistakable sex appeal that oozed from her very pores. It was in every move she made, every expression she gave, in her deep, sultry, sexy voice. He hadn't cared what she said to him, so long as she was talking.

"I said borrow money from Dad." His brother Matias spoke up from where he sat on a padded chair on the deck of Rafe's house, overlooking Pine Valley.

The sun was setting now on the western horizon, yellow, pink and wild-rose red painting the distant storm clouds. The temperature was August-hot, but an evening breeze brought some relief as Rafe arrived back from his beer run to the kitchen.

"You know I'm never going to do that." He set an icy bottle of beer down for his brother on the small round table, then took the chair on the opposite side, his own cold beer slick from condensation in his hand.

"Too proud?" Matias asked.

"Too practical." Rafe was also too proud, but that wasn't the most salient reason for his decision. "I promised myself RCW would make it on its own. I'm not liquidating my assets to prop it up, and I'm not asking anyone in the family for money, either."

"The embezzlement is just a temporary setback," Matias said.

"Maybe so. But I made the decision to invest in Soiree on the Bay."

"You and half the businesses in town."

Rafe took a pull on his beer. "It's like being in Vegas."

"Huh?"

"You set your limit going in, and you don't deviate from it even if the losses mount up."

Matias shot him a puzzled look. "You set a limit in Vegas? How is that any fun?"

Rafe chuckled. His brother might be the most reckless of the Cortez-Williams brothers, but he'd never let himself lose big in Vegas.

"Seriously," Matias said. "If you're going to gamble, gamble. It's not gambling if nothing meaningful is at stake."

"You're telling me you've lost real money in Vegas?"

Now Matias looked affronted. "Of course not." He snorted out a laugh. "I *win* in Vegas. But sad to say, I haven't been to Sin City in months."

"You betting on anything locally?"

"I'd bet on you," his brother said with all sincerity.

Rafe shook his head. "I don't need your money."

"You just said RCW is in serious financial trouble."

"It is. But we'll work it out with corporate resources. That's the deal I made with myself when I walked away from the ranch. Maybe we'll find Billy and get the money back."

"Given what I've heard about the scheme? Doubtful. That's a guy who's been thinking about this for a long time."

"I suppose," Rafe said. "What do you think does that to a man?"

"Sucks his conscience from his soul?"

"Yeah." That was pretty much what Rafe meant.

"Well, it looks like he's probably an Edmond."

Rafe chuckled at that, taking another drink, the effervescent liquid feeling good on his throat in the sultry evening. "You're saying the flaw is in the genetics?"

"Rusty's a cutthroat. Look what he did to his son Ross when he went against him."

Rafe gave his brother a mocking look. "You watched me walk out on Dad. Are you saying we're genetically tainted?"

"You and Dad didn't have *that* kind of a fight."

"It took us a while." Rafe's father considered the ranch his sons' heritage and their obligation, all five of them.

"But you got there," Matias said, gesturing again with his beer bottle for emphasis.

"We got there." Rafe's relationship with his father was a bit of an armed truce, but they were working on it. Still, he couldn't help but wonder what he'd be in

BARBARA DUNLOP   25

for if RCW failed. The *I-told-you-so*s from his father would be unrelenting.

"You were too cocky," Matias said.

"I was younger. No. Scratch that. I'd do the same today."

"Even knowing how it ends?"

"It hasn't ended."

"Especially if you let me lend you some money. Or buy in. I could be your partner. Sell me half of RCW."

Rafe burst out laughing at that. "You're not cut out for the restaurant business. Besides, can you imagine Dad coming unglued if you announced you were throwing in with me? Your horse breeding sideline is bad enough." Rafe shook his head. "Plus, you're a rancher, Matias, you and Lorenzo both."

"And you're not?" His brother looked disappointed as he asked.

"I'm not. I mean, I can rope and ride, run a herd, and pick cattle at auction. But I don't love it like you guys do."

"You love the restaurant business?" It was clear Matias couldn't understand that.

"I do." At least Rafe relished the day-to-day running of RCW, the enthusiasm of the staff, the joy of the customers having celebrations, the creativity of JJ and the other chefs.

He wasn't so wild about the Royal business community. They seemed to prefer the Cortez-Williams brothers as ranchers, slightly on the outskirts, not smack-dab in the middle of their corporate world. The ostracism was subtle, but he was still struggling to be accepted as a fully functioning member of the business community.

"To each his own," Matias said. "Hope you can hang on to it."

"I do, too."

There was a meeting of the Royal Chamber of Commerce this week to discuss a way out of the financial debacle for the chamber, the TCC and the whole town. Rafe was going to be there, and he was going to put his shoulder to the collective solution, whatever it was.

Gina came early to the Royal Chamber of Commerce meeting. She wanted to get seated before too many people arrived—ideally somewhere near the back, where the accusatory gazes of her fellow community members couldn't easily find her. It was no fun being a pariah.

For as long as she could remember, she'd been greeted warmly at TCC events and other happenings in Royal, first as a child and a teenager accompanying her father and other family members, but in recent years on her own, acknowledged as an Edmond in her own right.

However, today, she was slinking quietly in and trying to hide in the background.

Lila Jones was at the front of the room leaning over a rectangular table, the only person there so far. She looked up as Gina entered through the double doors at the back.

"Hi, Gina." Lila's expression was welcoming, her voice friendly. Then again, she had always been a decent person. A little understated maybe, before her recent makeover, but a solid, hardworking, respected member of the Royal business community.

Gina tried to imagine Lila being treated as a pariah. She couldn't. No matter what Lila's family did or didn't do, she would be respected for herself and her own accomplishments.

Gina wanted that for herself.

Her footsteps were muted on the carpet as she decided to make her way forward. "Can I help?" she asked the other woman.

"Help?"

"Anything to get ready?" It was a small offer, an insignificant offer really.

Normally, she would pour herself a coffee at the refreshment table or help herself to a bottle of water, sit down with friends and have a nice chat while the meeting got under way. This was the first time she'd considered the work that went into convening a chamber gathering.

Gina supposed it was Lila's job to put the meetings together. But the Royal Chamber of Commerce was primarily a volunteer organization, and it had never occurred to her to volunteer.

Lila glanced around, seemingly puzzled by Gina's offer. "I…uh…guess you could put out the agenda packages. I mean, if you don't mind."

"Not at all." Gina spotted a stack of agendas on the table. She tucked her purse snugly under her arm and picked up the stack.

"Thanks," Lila said.

"It's nice to have something to do."

Lila gave Gina a sympathetic smile, and started to say something, but then shut her mouth.

"What?"

"Nothing." Lila shook her head.

"Go ahead." Gina was curious.

"I'm just…sorry for what you're going through."

"It's been hard on the family."

"Not the family," Lila said. "You. Personally. It can't be fun having everyone staring and whispering behind your back."

Gina looked down at the agendas for a second. She wasn't used to pity. There'd never been a need for it in her life.

"I'm learning to cope," she admitted.

"That which doesn't kill us…" Lila let the famous quote fall away.

"Oh, I hope this makes me stronger," Gina said.

"Do you want it to make you stronger?" The other woman seemed sincere.

"I do."

"How're you going to do that?" Mere moments into the conversation, Lila had hit on the crux of the problem.

"Honestly? I have no idea. I usually just go along for the ride." As Gina said the words, she realized how very true they were. "How can that be?"

"You are who you are." Lila looked intelligent now, insightful, reminding Gina how she had always excelled in school. A grade ahead, while Gina and her friends were fussing about clothes and makeup and boys, Lila had been busy pulling in top marks, working hard, like she still seemed to be doing even after making a splash on social media.

Gina had never envied Lila. But she did now. Lila pulled her own weight in the world. It obviously gave her independence and self-worth.

"I don't want to be who I am," Gina impulsively admitted.

"Who do you want to be?"

Gina almost said *you*. "Someone who helps." She looked down at the agendas and laughed at herself, because she was standing here talking instead of getting to work. "But you've given me something to think about. Thank you." She began to step away to put the pamphlets on the tables, but then stopped and looked back. "Can I ask you something?"

"Sure."

Gina heard voices behind her and realized the other attendees were starting to arrive. She had to talk fast. "This thing you did."

"The *thing*?"

"Changing from studious to glam."

"I wouldn't say—"

"I want to do the opposite. I'm all glam all the time. I want to undo some of it. I want people to take me seriously. *You* are such a great balance."

There were more voices now, chatting together, calling to one another, chairs moving, people settling. Gina hated the thought of turning around to face them, but she was determined to pass out the agendas. It was a tiny thing, but it felt like a turning point.

"How about we chat over lunch?" Lila suggested. "One day this week?"

"That would be great." Gina took a bracing breath and turned to the room.

She kept everyone in her soft focus as she moved, not meeting any of the stares she knew were following her, ignoring the indistinct conversations that were probably about her and her family, focusing instead on the royal blue tabletops where she was depositing the agendas.

Finally, she finished, ending in a back corner of the room. She quickly sat down in a chair against the wall.

"Hello, Gina."

She didn't have to look over to recognize Rafe's voice. She'd definitely picked the wrong table.

Rafe couldn't help but admire Gina's moxie as she sat down next to him and his brother Lorenzo. But one look at her stricken expression told him it was an accident.

He waited to see what she'd do. Would she get up and flee, or would she stick it out?

"Hello, Rafe," she said. "Lorenzo." Her lips thinned and her posture straightened, but she made no move to switch to another table.

Her brother Ross Edmond walked in then. He scanned the room like he owned the place, which he practically did, the Edmond family being founding members of both the TCC and the Royal Chamber of Commerce.

When Ross spotted Gina, he was clearly confused by her choice of location. The Edmonds were front-and-center kind of people. He was probably puzzled by her table companions as well. He scanned Rafe and Lorenzo for a moment, then walked over to sit next to his sister.

"Hi, Lorenzo, Rafe. Hey, Gina." He gave her a half hug where she sat.

Asher Edmond entered the room and reacted the same way as his stepbrother, Ross, doing a double take of where his family was sitting.

Rafe could only imagine what was going to happen when patriarch Rusty Edmond walked in. He'd probably move the whole family to some better real estate near the front of the room, as was their due. The family might be persona non grata in the eyes of many business owners, but Rusty was unlikely to let that slow him down.

For now, Asher sauntered over. There were only four chairs at each table, set over half the round so everyone was facing front. Asher commandeered a chair from the next table, dragging it over next to Ross.

"Lorenzo, Rafe. How you guys doing?"

"Fine," Rafe said, although he was anything but, and these three people were at least in part to blame for that.

"Hey, Asher," Lorenzo said. "Welcome back to the world."

Asher gave a half smile at the joke. "Good to be back. Valencia didn't come out?"

Lorenzo shook his head. "She's with the horses. She's shorthanded right now."

Rafe knew Valencia Donovan had been counting on a share of the ticket sales from Soiree on the Bay. Her charitable horse rescue organization was strapped for cash now that the event had fallen through.

"Hopefully something good will come out of tonight," Asher said with a gaze around the filling room. "Heaven knows we all need it."

Lorenzo nodded his agreement.

"Can I have your attention, please?" Lila asked over the microphone.

The stragglers finished picking up cups of coffee and moved to their seats, while the conversation in the room settled down. Rafe couldn't help a surreptitious glance in Gina's direction. But when he met Ross's gaze, he looked away. The other man had to be used to guys eyeballing his sister, and Rafe wasn't about to be one of them, even if it *was* tempting.

"I'll officially call the meeting to order," Lila continued. "As you can see, there's only one item under new business tonight. And the minutes from the last meeting are attached. Will someone move to approve the minutes?"

A voice came from the far side of the room. "I'll move."

"Thank you. Anyone second?"

Ross closed his package and put up his hand. "Second."

"The minutes are so approved. Now on to new business. As you all know, the Royal Chamber of Commerce was a supporter of Soiree on the Bay rather than an investor. And while we can't be involved in any criminal probes or investigations, what we can do is facilitate a discussion on ideas for recouping some of your losses. We've been made aware that local businesses are struggling, and we hope this will be an opportunity for everyone to work collaboratively on viable solutions."

"What are the Edmonds going to do about it?" someone shouted out.

"Where are they?" said another.

"Hiding in the back corner."

There was swiveling in seats and turning of heads until all gazes were focused their way.

Gina shifted in her own seat, and Rafe felt sorry for her. Clearly, she'd chosen to sit back here to stay out of the fray. That clearly hadn't worked out for her.

"Where's Rusty?" someone called out as sidebar conversations arose around the room.

"Shouting isn't going to help," Lila broke in. "We're looking for *constructive* solutions."

Ross came to his feet, and people quieted down, clearly curious.

"My brother, sister and I—" Ross began.

Rafe scanned the room, monitoring the expressions of the crowd as Ross spoke.

"—will be donating to a relief fund set up through the Chamber of Commerce for local businesses impacted by the festival cancellation."

"Cancellation?" someone bellowed out incredulously.

"How much?" another person demanded.

Rafe could see the crowd wasn't softening toward the Edmonds. They were still suspicious and hostile. He didn't blame them. Because he felt the same way himself. In fact, he hoped nobody interpreted him and Lorenzo sitting at this table as being an implicit endorsement of the Edmonds.

"Together, we lost millions," someone else pointed out. "You gonna donate millions?"

"We can't cover it all," Ross admitted gruffly.

Everyone started talking at once.

"Please," Lila tried again through the microphone. She was doing a valiant job of trying to keep order.

"We're not saying it's the complete solution." Ross's voice rose. "We're just saying we want to do our part."

The crowd kept shouting out.

"I'm about to lose my business."

"Forget your business, my house is at stake."

"I've lost a year's worth of profits."

"I don't know if I can recover from this!"

Gina shifted in her seat, and Rafe checked out her expression, thinking she had to feel like she was under attack along with her brother. Protective instincts welled up inside him, even though it was none of his concern.

To his surprise, she didn't look intimidated. In fact, she looked determined. She put her hand on Ross's arm.

He glanced down at her, clearly taken aback when she rose to her feet.

"Let me," she whispered to him.

It was easy to see he was about to refuse.

"Please," she implored.

After a moment, he sat down.

The move surprised the crowd enough to quiet them down.

Her voice was slightly shaky as she started talking. "I'm not going to say I understand," she began. "But I will say that the best thing we can do here tonight is brainstorm some fundraising ideas. I get that it's satisfying to complain, and I know you're all looking for someone to blame."

Rafe could see that statement was a mistake even if she couldn't. The expressions of the crowd changed, and they looked like they were about to start shouting again.

"And maybe we are," Gina said in a clear, ringing voice. "But that won't help tonight. It won't help any of you get your money back. We need fundraising ideas."

Surprisingly the crowd settled again.

"That's a very productive suggestion," Lila said. "What about standard things, a walkathon, bowl-athon or read-athon."

"We could sell T-shirts," someone shouted.

"A white elephant sale?"

"Those are all local," Gina said. "We can't depend on local dollars this time."

There were nods around the room on that point.

"What about a talent show?" Lexi suggested.

"You mean a festival lite?" someone scoffed.

"We'd need a really big name to get any traction at all on social media," Abby Carmichael pointed out.

Lila spoke up again, sounding disheartened. "Big names won't want to be associated with Soiree on the Bay."

"What about services?" Gina asked. "What do we do here in Royal that's unique and valuable?"

"A bake sale?" someone asked.

"Too small-time," another person answered.

Rafe had an industrial kitchen, but he didn't see a bake sale—or any other fundraising suggestions that had been brought up so far—providing the kind of cash they needed.

Lexi's idea had been the best of the bunch, but only if they could get a big name, which they couldn't. No way, no how was any A-list performer going to touch Royal and Soiree on the Bay.

"We have beautiful scenery," someone said.

"Wide-open space."

"Cattle."

"Horses."

"Ranches!" Gina said, a thread of excitement in her voice.

"Sell a ranch?" someone asked incredulously.

"No. Not exactly." She started talking faster, her voice growing more animated. "Just raffle the ranch experience. Better still, a cowboy experience. The entire South, no the entire *country* is full of big-city dwellers who have no idea what it's like to spend a day on a working ranch with a real cowboy." She glanced at Lorenzo and Rafe.

Uh-oh. Rafe didn't like where this was going.

"We do the auction online. We go national. Maybe the cowboys give a little video spiel to entice bidders. We could get some stills of the ranches, show them off.

Make it sound fun. Make it sound exciting. Lila, you're the social media expert." Gina paused.

Everyone shifted their attention to the front of the room where Lila stood at the microphone. "It's an… idea," she said, clearly trying to organize her thoughts. "Maybe it could work…"

"Who's going to volunteer for *that*?" a male voice asked. It was Tucker McCoy, sixty-eight years old and still riding his own range. "Video myself yapping about heifers and hog-tying, then take some city slicker onto the range and maybe get them hurt or killed?"

"There'd be liability," someone noted.

"We'd cover the insurance," Gina said.

Both her brothers swung their heads to gape at her.

"A rider on the Edmond corporate policy," she said. "We could donate that. And the flights to get here. We'd donate those, too." She glanced at both her brothers, who were staring at her in stunned surprise.

"The Edmond family was already planning to donate to the cause. This could be part of the package. We add a high-end dinner to each experience, an outdoorsy day followed by a five-star evening." She put some cajoling humor into her voice. "If the cowboys are handsome, all the better."

"You still need willing cowboys," someone observed.

From the podium, Lila looked expectantly around the room. "Any volunteers?" she asked.

Nobody spoke up.

Rafe had to hand it to Lila, she was willing to make them all sweat it out. He had to give Gina props, too, for standing there with her idea crashing and burning in front of the whole town. Turning, he took a quick glance at her face, and saw her brave smile but also the trepidation in her eyes. He felt a spike of pity.

Aw, hell.

He came to his feet. "I'll do it," he said.

Lorenzo looked astonished.

Rafe motioned to his brother with his head, *get up*, being the clear message.

Lorenzo gave an imperceptible shake.

Rafe came back with a glare.

But before Lorenzo could stand, Tucker McCoy stood. "I'll do it, too," he said. "Don't see why a pretty gal wouldn't want to spend a day with me. I got more exciting stories than any of you young cowpokes."

"I'll volunteer Matias," Lorenzo called out.

More men stood, and the joking began.

Gina's shoulders drooped in obvious relief.

Three

Gina's brothers stayed silent until they were halfway across the chamber parking lot and out of earshot of the other meeting attendees.

"*What* was that?" Asher demanded.

"We *had* a plan," Ross added.

"Our plan wasn't working." Gina knew she'd gone way off script, but the crowd was turning on Ross, and she'd felt like she had to do something to help.

Ross stopped next to his car. "I can't imagine what Dad's going to say about this."

The three of them formed a small circle to continue the conversation.

Gina couldn't imagine what her father was going to say, either. "If he cares so much, he should have come out to the meeting," she boldly stated.

"Is *that* what you're going to tell him?" Asher asked.

Gina had hoped they'd talk to him together about the auction and their financial pledges to the cause. She wasn't afraid of Rusty, but she was intimidated by him. She always had been. "I'll tell him we're hoping to recoup some of the town's losses. That's a positive."

"I'm not sure he's in the mood for a positive," Ross ventured as vehicles started up around them, headlights sweeping as people pulled out for home, a few curiously craning their necks to look at the Edmonds as they passed.

"Rusty's not thinking straight on any front," Asher added. "He's raging at everyone right now."

"He has a right to be mad at Billy," Ross said.

"Maybe," Gina offered, not feeling a whole lot of sympathy or respect for her father given the revelations about his infidelity. "But you also have a right to be mad at him," she said to Ross.

Ross nodded. "I know. But it's hard to stay angry and be so happy at the same time."

"I admire your capacity for forgiveness." She wasn't sure she'd have done the same.

Ross had almost lost his child and the love of his life because of Rusty's machinations.

"Charlotte's the forgiving one," he said. "Dad has her to thank for that—Mom, too." He gave his head a shake. "After all she went through."

Gina understood the reconciliation with their mother more easily, since Sarabeth had been wronged by Rusty, too. "Has Dad thanked her?"

"In his way," Ross said.

"That man," she said through gritted teeth. "He almost sent Asher to jail."

"I did go to jail," Asher said ruefully. "But I got out again."

"We should have trusted you from the start," Gina said more softly, regretting that she'd ever doubted her stepbrother's innocence.

"Billy did a damn good job of framing me," Asher said. Then he gave Gina a playful bump with his shoulder. "If I didn't know for sure it wasn't me, I might have been swayed by the evidence."

"We were wrong about you," Ross said with regret.

"Water under the bridge," Asher stated. "And besides, we've got bigger problems than regret right now."

Ross shook his head, his attention going back to Gina. "I can't believe you went rogue on us back there."

"I think it's going to work," she said, feigning a confidence she wasn't feeling. They'd have to ramp up interest in the cowboy experience auction, get some attention on social media, and hope and pray that city people with deep pockets would be excited to fly to Texas.

Ross's tone was fatalistic. "I guess we'll all find out together."

"Thanks for the vote of confidence," she deadpanned, taking out her key as she prepared to head for her car on the other side of the parking lot.

There was a glass of brandy at home with her name on it. If she could make it through the mansion undetected by her father and whatever industry or political VIPs he was collaborating with tonight, she might just wrangle an hour of peace and quiet on her balcony overlooking the pool.

"I better get home to Lani," Asher said.

"Night," Gina murmured to her brothers, before turning to make the walk to her metallic blue convertible.

As she approached with her fob, the lock on her car clicked open automatically. She then caught sight of

Rafe angling his way to an SUV two stalls down. Gina knew she should thank him for supporting her on the auction, so she stopped and waited.

He slowed as he came up to her.

"Thanks," she said. "You didn't have to do that." In fact, she was still surprised that he had.

He wasn't even a rancher anymore, but he'd stepped up when nobody else was willing, getting the ball rolling instead of leaving her standing there.

His broad shoulders came up in a shrug beneath his nicely cut business suit. "Somebody had to do something."

"To help with the fundraising." That made sense.

"To save the princess from public humiliation."

His words shocked her to silence. What an appalling thing to say when she was trying to be polite.

"You're too accustomed to the free ride," he elaborated.

"Excuse me?" If he was so resentful of her, why had he even offered to help?

"You're used to people loving you unconditionally, so you go boldly forward wherever the muse takes you."

"I am *not*." Sure, she'd grown up in privilege, but she wasn't naive. She thought about her actions before she took them—all the time.

"Ah, Princess." He shook his head.

"Quit calling me that."

"Then quit being one."

"You act like I'm spoiled when I'm stepping up. I'm taking the lead to solve the problem," she pointed out.

"You call that taking the lead?"

"What else would you call it?"

"Suggesting an elaborate idea off the cuff."

"It was a *good* idea." She regretted stopping to thank him for his help. The big jerk sure didn't deserve it.

"It wasn't a *terrible* idea," he conceded.

"Well, I didn't hear you suggest anything better." When he didn't answer, she felt emboldened.

"And *my* idea turned out to be the best."

He gave a slow smile at her declaration. "Were you also teacher's pet?"

She tensed. "Why are you criticizing me?"

"Because no one ever has. It was an idea, Gina. It's a decent idea. But it's going to take a whole lot more than the flicker inside your brain to pull this off."

"I never said I was finished." She got that there was more to do. She wasn't exactly sure how that more would happen, but that was step two.

"Yeah?" he said, widening his stance. "What are you going to do next?"

"I'm going…" Her mind started to work. They'd need liability insurance. A venue to hold the auction. And they'd need—

"Yes?" he prompted.

"Cowboys," she said, confident in her decision. "We need more cowboys to increase the profits." Only ten had volunteered tonight.

"Where are you going to get them?"

Ha. She had an answer for that. "The TCC."

"Your daddy's out of favor with the members right now."

She was insulted again. "I'm not running to my father for help."

"You've lost your sheen at the TCC, too. Your whole family has. And a lot of those TCC guys don't even have working ranches anymore."

She leaned in, challenging him. "Are you going to stand there and shoot down all of my ideas?"

"I'm trying to help."

"Is *that* what you call it?"

He shifted slightly closer, and she picked up his woodsy scent. His big, tall form was imposing, his face ruggedly handsome, with that chiseled chin and the shadow of a beard, and those deep dark eyes that made his mood a mystery.

She would have guessed he was angry, but an energy also lurked in their depths. It looked more like excitement than ire. But maybe she was projecting. Because she was excited—no, *aroused*. And that wasn't good.

"I want you to succeed," he said, pulling her off the emotional tangent. It was frighteningly easy to get lost in Rafe's magnetism.

"By insulting me?" she asked.

"By grounding you in the real world."

"I'm grounded."

He chuckled at that. The rich sound cascaded around her, amplifying her attraction and threatening to distract her from the argument again.

She caught herself just in time. "Have you paid *any* attention for the last few weeks?"

His expression hardened, shadowed by the overhead light. "Believe me, Princess, I've paid plenty of attention."

"Then you know what I've been through."

"This isn't about you."

She stumbled over that. Gina knew his business was in trouble, and she hadn't meant to imply it was about her. She was trying to fix the problem, for all of them.

Rafe stepped even closer. "Take *that* as a lesson."

While she didn't exactly understand, she didn't want to admit it. So instead, she stood her ground while her brain struggled for a cogent response and her hormones galloped off with unbridled attraction.

He had a confident tilt to his chin, a hungry gleam in his eyes, but a softness to his full lips—especially the lower one—that made them kissable, *highly* kissable.

He bent slightly forward, then stopped. A heartbeat went by, and she could almost feel his hot lips graze hers. But then he straightened instead. He stepped back, and his words sounded far away. "Let me know if I can help some more."

She shook herself back to reality and to the unmistakable feeling she'd been bested at something. She couldn't quite put her finger on what.

"Uh…okay." It was the best she could come up with on the fly, her hormones still clouding her brain.

He seemed to focus on her forehead as he took another step away. "Night, Gina."

"Good night."

He turned for his vehicle then, long strides taking him effortlessly away.

She watched his smooth gait, firming her own legs beneath her, struggling to ascertain how he'd so easily hijacked her hormones and used them against her.

Then he paused at the driver's door and turned, looking back at her one more time as the night wind brushed her heated skin.

Rafe couldn't put his finger on what had happened last night. One minute he was teasing Gina Edmond about her ineptitude and inexperience, the next he was headed in for a kiss and fighting a sudden startling desire to haul her into the back seat of his SUV and—

"So, you just stood there and *let* him?" Matias's question brought Rafe back to the present as the two men crossed the RCW Steakhouse patio.

Rafe set the two Tex-Mex omelets he'd cooked up in the RCW kitchen on a dining table by the rail that bordered one of the town's greenbelts. The restaurant didn't open for another three hours, and it was still comfortably cool outside. Maples and oak trees dotted the lush grass and would shade the tables once afternoon rolled around.

Rafe sat on a padded chair, settling in. "He didn't stop to ask me before he did it."

Matias sat across from him, dropping utensils in the middle of the table and setting a steaming cup of coffee in front of each of them. "He had no right to just up and volunteer me."

"You got something better to do?" Rafe told himself he didn't care if his brother participated in the auction or not.

Gina would be disappointed, sure. But it wasn't up to Rafe to keep Gina Edmond happy, even if she did have the greatest smile west of New Orleans, or maybe it was west of Miami, probably even Rome.

"Yes," Matias said.

"Like what?"

Matias cut into his omelet. "Plenty of things—horse training, irrigation, tractor maintenance."

"We haven't even picked a date."

"It doesn't matter the date. I'm busy. Tell her no."

"Me? You tell her no." Not that Rafe wanted to give up a chance to see Gina again.

"I'm not good around pretty women." Matias took a bite of the omelet.

For some reason, Rafe was hit with a jolt of jealousy. "Pretty?"

Matias swallowed, then lifted his tall black coffee mug with the stylized RCW logo. "We *are* talking about Gina Edmond, right?"

"Yes." There was no other.

Matias gave a gesture with the cup that clearly said *then what are you talking about?*

His brother was right.

"You're fine around pretty women," Rafe said instead.

"If I'm making them happy, sure." A sly gleam came into Matias's eyes. "It's when I'm disappointing them—"

"And I *know* you've had plenty practice at that." With a satisfied grin, Rafe put a bite of the spicy omelet in his mouth, enjoying the results of his efforts. He was nowhere near JJ's caliber, but he could whip up a mean omelet.

"You'd know more about disappointing them than me," Matias retorted.

"No complaints," Rafe said. "Well, maybe a few complaints." With a self-deprecating grin, he took a swig of his hot coffee.

Matias chuckled.

"Just do it," Rafe said. "It'll take a day. Make a little money for the town. Show some community spirit."

His brother watched him for a moment. "You still feel it, don't you?"

"Feel what?"

"That you're not really one of them, not good enough,

don't fit into the business leaders' clique in the chamber."

"I fit in fine," Rafe lied. "RCW is one of the top-rated, most successful restaurants in Royal. People come from Dallas for our T-bones, never mind the sambal shrimp. We had a write-up in *Southwestern Gourmet* just last month. They featured our cranberry apple pastry."

"Methinks the cowboy protests too much."

Rafe realized he had. "I was only making a point."

Matias's expression turned thoughtful, and he sobered. "Is that what you're so scared of losing?"

"I'm not scared." *Worried* was a better word.

But Matias kept following his line of thinking. "If the restaurant closes, you know you won't go personally bankrupt. And I don't think you care about Dad's opinion as much as you pretend you do."

"Would you want an I-told-you-so from Dad?"

"Nobody wants that." He was watching Rafe closely now. "But you can take it."

Rafe didn't like where this was leading, mostly because it was hitting close to home. He raised his voice for emphasis. "It's simple. I've put my heart and soul into this place. I don't want to lose my restaurant to bankruptcy."

Rafe caught a movement in the corner of his eye. He twisted his head to see JJ standing there.

"Sorry, boss," the chef said, turning to go. But there was no way he could have missed Rafe's statement.

"You heard that," Rafe said.

JJ looked back, disheartened. He nodded.

Rafe gave in to the inevitable. "Come and join us. Grab a coffee."

Matias exchanged a look with Rafe while JJ got himself a cup of coffee.

"He didn't know?" Matias asked unnecessarily.

"I was going to have to tell him sometime."

"Man," Matias said on the whoosh of a breath. He knew JJ was one of the foundational staff members at RCW. He'd worked almost as hard as Rafe to ensure its success. And unlike Rafe, JJ relied on a regular paycheck to support his mother and his extended family.

"I'm not going to let it happen," Rafe said to JJ as he sat down between them.

"But it's possible?" JJ asked, twisting his cup back and forth.

Matias took another bite of his omelet.

"Yes," Rafe admitted. "But the whole town's trying to dig everyone out of the financial hole."

"Even the Edmonds?" JJ asked, knowing as everyone else did that the Edmonds' fortune was legendary. "Will they take an equity stake in RCW?" He frowned at that. "It's none of my business, Rafe, but I don't think you want to get tangled up with that family."

"I'd listen to JJ," Matias chimed in.

"I'm not going into business with the Edmonds," Rafe stated firmly. Giving up a piece of RCW would be his very last choice of a solution. And Rusty Edmond was reputed to be cutthroat in business. "They're fundraising and donating to the cause. To start, there's an auction coming up."

"And that's where I came in," Matias said, setting down his fork, clearly preparing to leave.

"An auction?" JJ asked.

"It might be workable, and it might not." Rafe didn't really trust Gina to pull it off on her own, never mind turn it into the kind of marquee event they'd need to raise a serious amount of money. "A *cowboy experience* auction."

"With genuine ranchers," Matias put in with disgust. He pointed to himself and to Rafe. "Local sacrificial lamb cowboys who are apparently required to humiliate themselves on the auction block."

JJ ventured a little grin as he glanced between the two men. "Luckily, my Malaysian heritage is in fishing."

"You grew up in Maverick County," Matias said.

"Not on horseback," JJ countered.

"You're worrying way too much about doing it," Rafe said to his brother. "Chill. It'll take one day, tops."

"Will it help recoup our losses?" JJ asked.

"Yes," Rafe said, silently hoping so.

"Then saddle up, cowboy," JJ told Matias. "We've got a business to save."

Gina was pondering Rafe's advice, even though he'd given it sarcastically. She'd sat out on her bedroom balcony and thought through the mechanics of pulling off an auction. And to her consternation, she'd come up with about a hundred moving parts.

Her degree was in business administration with a major in marketing. But she'd never had to put any of her skills to use. She came home from college to a guaranteed job in the family oil company with an executive assistant, a spacious office and very little work to do. She'd eventually fallen into the habit of reading company reports, attending board meetings, taking long lunches and asking very few questions, since her father kept an iron grip on operations, they had excellent employees, and the company was thriving without her participation.

Since she'd never managed a real project before, she'd spent this entire morning strategizing a plan of action and then formulating a task list that had eventually frightened her, since about ten different things had to happen right away.

Resisting an urge to throw a dart to choose her starting point, she settled on Mandee Meriweather. The host of the celebrity gossip show, *Royal Tonight!*, was far from Gina's favorite TV personality, but she was popular and could bring the event some much-needed publicity.

She drove directly to the studio and approached the reception counter on the ground floor, giving the middle-aged woman sitting there a bright smile. "Good morning. I wanted to talk to someone about *Royal Tonight!*"

The receptionist gave her a critical up-and-down look.

Gina was wearing a lightweight sleeveless dress, pure white on top, snug in the bodice, with a kicky flared skirt in a flowing autumn leaf pattern that grew denser and bolder toward the hem. She'd paired it with classic cream-colored heeled sandals and a few pieces of plain gold jewelry, except for her earrings, which were a cascade of jade beads set in gold, nicely balancing the highlights of the leaves. Her brunette hair was left free and flowing, and she'd tucked her sunglasses on top of her head.

She had no idea why the woman was frowning.

"We don't directly hire talent," the receptionist said. "I'm not here—"

"Do you have an appointment?" the receptionist asked.

"No. I have a proposal for—"

"I'm sorry, you'll have to call for an appointment."

"Call?" Gina was standing right here.

"Or you can go to our website royaltonight-dot-com."

"To make an appointment?" Did the process need to be that convoluted?

"To submit your portfolio."

Gina calmed her annoyance. "I'm not here looking for a job. I'd like to make an appointment with whoever schedules shows for *Royal Tonight!*"

The woman heaved a heavy sigh. Then she extracted a business card and pushed it across the reception counter to Gina. "If you don't want to use the website, then call this number."

Gina heard the door open behind her. "You can't book me an appointment now?"

"All appointments are done through central booking." The receptionist's attention moved past Gina. "Can I help you with something?" She put on a welcoming smile to greet the new arrival.

Gina looked sideways to see a crisply dressed, serious-looking thirtysomething woman.

The woman handed the receptionist a business card. "I'm Taylor Millen from Kuntz and Walker. I was wondering if one of the marketing reps had time for a quick chat."

The receptionist picked up her phone and pressed a few buttons.

Ms. Millen gave Gina a nod, and Gina nodded back.

"Do you have time for a walk-in?" the receptionist asked into the phone. She waited a minute. "Thank you, Peter." She put down the phone and pointed to a hallway to the right of the reception area. "You can go right in. Third door on the left."

"Thank you so much," Taylor said before moving on her way.

The receptionist looked back at Gina, her expression making it clear she wondered why Gina was still there.

She wondered that, too. Why was she still cooling her heels in the reception area? Was she not a walk-in? Maybe she needed a business card. Better still, she should get herself a no-nonsense navy blue suit and a pair of glasses.

She pocketed the card with the phone number and headed out to the sidewalk, deciding to give up on the receptionist and just call. Hopefully, she could book an appointment for today or tomorrow.

Three voice mail messages later, with no idea when they'd call back, Gina sat in her car, tapping her thumbs on the steering wheel. She'd blown most of her first morning on the auction project, and she had practically nothing to show for it.

She thought about cowboys. But that made her think about Rafe. She didn't want to think about Rafe, especially after their near-kiss last night...

She shook the image of him from her mind, backing further up in the evening to her conversation with Ross and Asher. But thinking of Ross and Asher made her think about her father and how she hadn't yet told him about the auction. She promised herself she'd do that tonight, after dinner, after he'd had a bourbon or two. Then she moved on.

Her next thought was of Lila, and she knew she was

onto something useful. The woman would be her next stop. Gina pushed the button to start her car.

Ten blocks and one pit stop at Angelo's Pizzeria later, she was pulling into the Chamber of Commerce parking lot. She went through the main entrance to reception, hoping to find Lila in her office.

It was nearing one o'clock and the admin area was empty, but she found Lila's open office door and knocked.

Lila looked up from her computer and seemed surprised. "Gina?"

Gina gave an apologetic smile and held up the large pizza box and two soft drinks. "Lunch?" she asked.

Lila pushed back from her computer, beaming then. "A woman after my own heart."

"I'm here to pick your brain," she admitted. "I hope you don't mind."

"Does that pizza have pepperoni on it?"

"The works, plus extra cheese."

"Then my brain is all yours." Lila gestured to a small round table in the corner of her office. She cleared away a few files and put them on her desk. "Smells amazing."

Gina set the pizza box in the middle of the table and peeled back the lid.

Lila helped herself to a slice and they each opened a soda. "So, what's up?"

"Two questions," Gina said while Lila took a bite, then made a comical face of ecstasy.

Her phone rang, but she waved it off and swallowed. "It'll go to voice mail. Go ahead."

"First, what would my authority be to organize and execute the auction?"

"Good question. I mean, nobody really said at the

meeting. But it *was* your idea. And you're arranging the liability insurance." Lila shrugged. "I'd say, go for it."

"You're saying nobody'll stop me if I take the helm?"

"I don't see why they would."

Gina chalked that one up as a win. She lifted a slice of the gooey pizza, looking forward to diving in. "Then, second, I need people to take me seriously."

"Who's not taking you seriously?"

Voices sounded in the reception area as people obviously returned from lunch.

"Hang on a second." Lila rose to close the door. Then she returned to sit back down.

The two women ate and drank in silence for a few minutes before they got down to business.

"So, who needs to take you seriously?" Lila asked as she went in for a second slice.

"I went down to the *Royal Tonight!* studio this morning. I thought we could get Mandee Meriweather to MC the auction."

"That's a really good idea."

"I couldn't get past the receptionist." Gina rolled her eyes. "She thought I was an actress looking for a job."

Lila took in Gina's outfit. "That's because you're so pretty."

Gina knew it was more than that. "You're pretty, maybe prettier than me. *Lots* of women are pretty. But everyone respects you."

Lila seemed to consider. "Maybe it's a glam thing. You've got a flare, a style."

"So do you."

"My glam look is really new." Gina recalled how Lila had undergone a transformation this summer as she became active on social media.

"I was thinking I should get a pair of glasses."

"You need glasses?" the other woman asked.

"No. They'd be clear, but they'd give me, you know, an intellectual look."

"Maybe," Lila said, tilting her head sideways as she considered Gina. "But I think it's more of an attitude."

"Could you teach me that? The attitude?" Gina wiped her glistening fingertips on her paper napkin.

"Okay…here's the thing." Lila rocked her head, like she was thinking hard. "Am I going to insult you?"

Gina braced herself. "Go ahead…give it to me with both barrels. No, wait!" She took another slice of pizza. "Okay. Now."

Lila laughed. "It's not how you look. Okay, it's a little bit how you look. I wouldn't get glasses. I might rethink the dress and the earrings—for the purpose of business, that's all. They look *great* on you. But maybe separates? Or solid colors?"

Gina nodded. She could do that…and wouldn't even need to go shopping. Her closet was full of all kinds of different pieces, some she'd never worn.

"Attitude, too. How do I say this? Don't depend on… guys wanting to buy you a drink."

Gina drew back, a little bit insulted. "I don't try to get men to buy me drinks."

"But they do."

Yeah, Gina would admit that, always of their own volition. But she nodded again.

"You've spent your whole life being charming."

"And nothing else?" Gina guessed that's how the sentence ended.

Lila gave a grimace. "Yeah, here's the part where I might insult you."

"Wait. We haven't gotten there yet?" Now Gina really braced herself.

"It's more what you do."

"I haven't done anything."

Lila grimaced again.

Oh, ouch. "And it shows."

"Not so much shows in that people can see it on you, but you don't have a reputation for getting things done. You haven't built up credibility, made connections, gained people's trust."

"Too busy being charming, huh?"

Lila shrugged. "Too busy doing what's worked for you your whole life. Nobody blames you for that."

"It sounds like you do."

Now it was Lila who looked like she was bracing herself.

"No," Gina said. "I'm not mad. I'm…disappointed, in *me*. Because you're right."

"You succeeded in your world, probably because you're smart. But if you want to succeed in a different world—and that's what I'm hearing—you need to be smart in a different way. Stop depending on your charm and your looks and your family connections. Hone some of your other tools."

Gina considered what those tools might be. "I took a project management course in college. I can write a critical path."

"That's good. But there's one particular best-in-class, beats-everything tool you'll need."

Gina was all ears. "What's that?"

"Hard work."

"But, I do—" Gina cut herself off. If she was already working hard, she wouldn't have this problem. And that was Lila's point. "Wow."

"You took that better than I thought," Lila said.

"I won't say it didn't pinch."

"You barely flinched."

"Hard work," Gina repeated, thinking the theory was so simple, but the execution would take work, and that work would be hard. She almost laughed at herself for the circular thinking.

"You just look around and pick up whatever needs doing."

"*Cowboys* are what needs doing." Gina grimaced. "Wait, that didn't come out right."

Lila laughed.

Gina elaborated. "First steps are to find enough cowboys for the auction. Also, to get Mandee Meriweather to agree to MC."

"You're off to the races," Lila said, giving a mock air toast with her slice of pizza. "Or, in this case, more like off to the roundup."

Four

Rafe heard Gina was failing miserably with the local cowboys. He got wind of the rumor from Lorenzo, then from Matias. Same story, two sources, only difference was that Matias was happy about the potential cancellation of the auction.

Rafe understood the business community was in trouble, and the ranchers were being asked to step up— again. He didn't think it was up to him to save Gina Edmond. But then he spotted her coming out of the *Royal Tonight!* studios looking dejected, like she'd just had something else go off the rails.

Questioning his own sanity, he swung his SUV into a parking spot at the sidewalk next to her shiny sports car.

She didn't look up, so he opened the driver's door and stepped outside to get her attention.

Gina saw him then and froze like a deer in the headlights.

He couldn't imagine why. Their last interaction had been spirited, sure, but it had also been fun, at least for him. He'd found himself attracted to her beyond her looks, which were obviously spectacular. But he also liked her spunk, her buoyant style, her intelligence and her ability to spar with him.

He'd wanted to kiss her that night, to kiss her and so much more, and he'd wanted it pretty bad. But she didn't know that. She wasn't a mind reader.

"Hey, Gina," he said, giving her a casual nod in greeting.

"Hi." She didn't move, so he shut his door and approached her, stepping up on the sidewalk.

"How's the auction coming along?" He knew the answer was "terrible," but he didn't want to let on that he'd been listening to gossip.

"I'm working hard," she said defensively.

He was sure she thought she was. And maybe that was the truth. She'd certainly approached a whole lot of ranchers the past couple of days.

He nodded to the *Royal Tonight!* studio. "Are they on board?"

She followed the direction of his gaze with her own. Her answer was subdued. "Not yet."

"Why not?"

She squared her shoulders like she was gearing up for battle dressed in her slim gray dress and fitted jacket. The outfit was adorned with matte silver buttons, giving it a slightly military air. Her hair was swept back in a loose knot revealing a pair of tiny twister-silver hoop earrings.

She tossed her head. "The small size of the event. At least that's what they claim."

"You need more cowboys to auction?" he guessed, going with logic as well as what he'd learned from his brothers.

"I've talked to most of the ranchers in Maverick County, even went over to Colonial. They're not willing to volunteer their property or their cowboys."

"Did you go dressed like that?" he asked.

She looked down at herself. "No. Not exactly. And what's wrong with this?"

"You look…"

"Professional?"

"Staid, uptight."

"No. I look *professional*," she told him archly. "I already went over this with Lila."

Rafe let the Lila comment slide, since it wasn't his central point, even though he was curious about what the other woman might have said. "They're ranchers, not bankers."

"I don't care who they are, looking competent and capable is important."

"So is looking approachable, respectful, like an actual human being."

Gina scowled at him. "Did you stop me just to insult me?"

"No. I stopped you to help you."

She let out a strangled laugh.

"When in Rome, Gina." He raised his eyebrow to drive home his point.

"I'm not going to pretend to be a rancher. Do you not think they'd see right through that?"

"I'm not saying fake anything. But with your pedigree, your…" He paused to frame the right words. "Bearing and attitude, when you march up to a rancher's front door looking like *this*, you can't expect them to give you the time of day." He realized his voice had grown louder and glanced around the quiet sidewalk to make sure no one had overheard.

She didn't respond, but she looked even more miserable.

"Gina."

"Is this you gloating?"

"No. It's me helping," he answered.

"You have a ridiculous way of helping."

"I'm being honest."

"You're being *insulting*."

He could see this was getting them nowhere. "What about this? Let me pick your wardrobe."

She opened her mouth to speak, but he bowled right over her. "And I'll come with you to see the ranchers, and we'll try again."

She shut her mouth, peering at him with suspicion.

"No trick," he assured her, holding his palms up. "I want this to work." He *did* want it to work—for him, for the other businesses, for Royal itself, and even for Gina.

"Why?" she asked.

"For the sake of Royal. Come on." He gestured to his SUV. "Let's find you a pair of blue jeans that cost something less than an average mortgage payment."

"My jeans don't cost—" She stopped mid-sentence, and her expression turned perplexed.

"You don't know the amount." It was both funny and sad at the same time. Rafe rounded to the passenger side of the vehicle and opened the door, gesturing her in.

"I…"

"Which of them eludes you?" He genuinely wanted

to know. "The cost of an average mortgage payment or the price of your blue jeans?"

She lifted her chin and marched his way. "Neither."

"Oh, Gina."

She paused beside him and looked up. "Don't *oh, Gina* me. I know things. They're just different things. And I'm still learning..."

She was too delightful for him to stay frustrated with for long. It was her superpower. Plus, he believed she truly was trying. A guy had to give her points for that.

Inside the SUV, he doubled back along Cedar Street and turned onto Silversmith Road.

"We're not going to the Courtyard Shops?"

"No, Princess."

"You want me to start calling you Cowpoke?"

Rafe shrugged. "Call me whatever you want."

"Okay, *Cowpoke*. I don't even know what you expect to find for clothes at this end of town."

Rafe knew exactly where he was going.

A few miles later, he pulled into the parking lot of a strip mall.

"Mama's Subs?" Gina read one of the signs. "Black Peak Appliance Repair? Sheila's Dog Grooming?" She turned to him. "Is there a joke in this somewhere?"

Rafe nodded directly in front of them.

Gina looked. "Second Chance Shelf?" The name sank in and her eyes went wide. *"What?"*

"You can't stagger up to a ranch house in a pair of brand-new blue jeans. They have to look lived-in."

"I'm not wearing someone else's clothes."

"Relax. They wash them before they resell them."

"No, Rafe. No freaking way. This is a showstopper for me."

He shut off the engine anyway. "You're *seriously* going to stop the show over this?"

"Yes."

"It's not like I'm asking you to ride a bull or eat a bug."

She slid her gaze his way. "Eat a bug?"

"The clothes are clean. They're fine. And you're wearing underwear." He paused then, taking in the flinch in her expression. "You are wearing underwear, right?"

"*Yes*, I'm wearing underwear." But the look on her face made him wonder just how flimsy that underwear might be.

He was forced to shake off several enticing images. "We don't have time for this."

"Good. Let's go."

"I mean, we don't have time to mess around. Businesses are getting more stressed by the day, and I can't see you keeping up the enthusiasm for this project forever. You need to sign up participants, nail Mandee down and find yourself a venue."

"We're using the Elegance Ranch."

That answer caught him off guard. "Does Rusty know?"

Gina's father was an intensely elitist and private person. Rafe couldn't see him agreeing to let his ranch be used for an auction that would be broadcast across the country, especially now with his family under such intense scrutiny.

"Not yet," she said.

"You are bold. And you're brave. And I can't believe you're going to let a little thing like wearing used blue jeans stop you from making this work." He had her with that argument. He *knew* he had her.

She gave him a glare, and he opened the driver's door, sliding out with the certainty that she'd follow.

She did.

Gina stared in the cracked and pitted sliver of a mirror inside the tiny changing cubicle of Second Chance Shelf.

"The red plaid is way too much," she called through the thin curtain.

"Show me," Rafe called back.

She whipped open the curtain to make her point. In the faded boyfriend-style blue jeans, the scuffed, tooled leather cowboy boots and the bright red plaid flannel shirt, she looked like someone from a sitcom.

She stepped out and spread her arms wide. "See?"

Rafe grinned. "It's not that bad."

"It's comical, satirical, mortifying."

"The shirt is a bit of overkill."

"A *bit*?"

"The jeans are okay." He walked around to look at her from other angles. "And the boots work."

The light brown leather boots were surprisingly comfortable, worn but not shabby, with low, blocky heels. It had been a while since she'd worn shoes that had this much stability. They'd be good for crossing gravel driveways and uneven pastures. The jeans were faded an attractive pale blue with white top stitching. They were loose in the calves, low-waisted, soft against her thighs even though she'd bet they didn't have a stitch of Lycra fabric to give them stretch.

"Try the one with the flowers," Rafe suggested.

He'd sent her into the changing room with four different shirts.

"The appliqué? No, thanks."

"It's cute."

"I'm not going for cute."

"Yes, you are."

She gave him a look that was half frown, half glare.

"They're cowboys, Gina, not critics at Fashion Week."

"What do you know about Fashion Week?"

"Enough to know it doesn't have Western wear."

"Fine." She'd decided humoring Rafe was her best move forward, so she gritted her teeth and did just that.

It was easy to see she wouldn't get any more local cowboys on board by herself. For better or worse, Rafe was her best bet to change their minds. And if she could recruit a few more cowboys, then she could get Mandee on board, and then she'd have a fighting chance of pulling this whole thing off.

She flounced back into the cubicle, pulled the curtain and stripped off the red shirt.

The flowered shirt felt like it was almost new. But the style was outrageous.

He gazed at her critically for a moment. "Let's call that plan B."

"Let's call it plan H."

"The snake print?" he suggested.

"I wasn't even going to try that one on."

"Come on. Be a sport."

"Fine. If only to prove you wrong."

"Go ahead. Prove me wrong. I dare you."

Back in the cubicle again, she stripped down to her cream-colored lace bra and slipped into the slinky fabric of the silver-and-blue snakeskin shirt. It felt embarrassingly supple against her skin, whisper-thin without being at all translucent.

She moved, twisting from one side to the other, watching the light play off the subtle pattern. She didn't *hate* it. She'd give it that.

"Come on out," Rafe called.

She pulled back the curtain.

He gazed for a moment. "Now all you need is a ponytail and we can have a little fun."

"Hard work," she muttered to herself as she turned in the mirrored, checking over her shoulder to see how it looked from behind. "But a critical path is a critical path."

"Did you just say I was on your critical path?" He was suddenly closer, and the timbre of his voice rumbled through her.

She turned and they came face-to-face. Her chest tightened as a now-familiar surge of desire rose within her.

"I said…" She lost her train of thought.

"Yeah?" he prompted. There was no denying the heat in his dark eyes.

She searched her brain for logic. "Cowboys." She landed on it. "Cowboys are on my critical path."

"I'm a cowboy." He quirked a half smile, and her desire ramped up further.

Did the man have to look so kissable?

"*New* cowboys…for the auction." She felt like she was subtly swaying his way, but she couldn't tell if it was an illusion.

"So, not me," he said. "At least not here. Not right now."

She didn't really understand the question. If it even *was* a question.

He touched the fabric at her shoulder, rubbing it between his fingertips. "Soft." Then his fingers rested lightly on her shoulder, warm through the fabric. "I want to kiss you, you know."

Gina had no response for that. She didn't want to say no, but she was afraid to say yes.

He brushed her cheek with the pad of his thumb. Then he glanced around at the other shoppers. "But that's going to have to wait."

Wait? As in, later? As in, he was planning to kiss her at some point in the future?

It seemed like something she should shut down right away, refuse to be drawn into. She should tell him a kiss between them wasn't going to happen now—or ever. But her focus was on his dark lips, imagining them against her own, hot, tender, probing.

Oh, man. This was going to be—

"So, we're agreed?" he asked.

"On the kiss?"

His grin went wide, flashing white with obvious amusement. "On the shirt."

Mortification suffused her. "Right." She swallowed then stepped back and turned away. "I'll go change."

His hand shot out to cup her shoulder.

She paused and looked back, and the air crackled between them.

"The kiss, too," he said with a meaningful lift of his brow.

Fourteen ranches and twenty cowboys later, Gina was beaming in the passenger seat as they whizzed back down the highway. Their windows were open and fresh wheatgrass-scented air billowed through the SUV.

Rafe was happy to be done and heading back to Royal. The sun was setting, and he had kissing Gina on his mind.

"That's thirty in all," she said, satisfaction in her voice.

It was odd, but she seemed to have grown into the casual clothes over the course of the day. She looked sexier than ever slouched down in the seat, wisps of her brunette hair blowing loose around her face.

"That sounds good," he said.

"It's the perfect number. There's some duplication in the ranches, sure. The Nester Ranch has three cowboys participating. But that place is huge. We'll be able to get a ton of different still shots to sell it on the website."

Rafe knew his presence had helped the effort. His family was familiar with everyone in the community. At some point in his life, he'd either worked with or partied with every rancher in both Maverick and Colonial Counties. The fact that he was enthusiastically participating in the auction had gone a long way toward boosting their confidence in the project.

But that didn't detract from Gina's effort. Once she'd calmed down a little and taken some of the intensity out of her pitch, she'd done well with the ranchers. They were great people, and invariably ready to step up for their neighbors.

"Two Cortez-Williams cowboys, too," he noted.

"I'll never forget that you were first."

He glanced momentarily her way. "I wasn't looking for gratitude."

"I know. But none of this would have happened without you. On both fronts."

"You did good back there," he told her honestly. "Once you relaxed."

"I was nervous. Some of those guys had already turned me down."

"But you got right back on the horse."

"I did." She gave a nod. "Mandee Meriweather will *have* to admit it's worthwhile now."

"That can wait until tomorrow." It was coming up on eight o'clock in the evening. "You hungry? We could stop in Joplin."

She sat up straight. "Ooh. Have you ever been to Custom Creekside?"

He gave her a sidelong look of incredulity. "You're asking a restaurant owner if he's checked out the competition?"

"When you put it that way…I guess you have."

"That's right. So you want to hop in the back seat and turn yourself into the real Gina?" He wasn't anxious for her to do that, but her dress and jacket were in the back of the SUV if she wanted to change for the upscale restaurant.

She seemed to hesitate.

"Or we could stop at the Twin Bears instead," he said.

"I've never been there."

Her answer didn't surprise him. "Burgers and milkshakes. All homemade, great stuff."

She pulled down the sun visor and checked out her face in the little mirror. "I'm definitely beyond repair."

She looked gorgeous to him.

"Twin Bears it is," she said, flipping the mirror back up.

Rafe was glad to hear that, because he wanted Gina to stay exactly the way she was.

Five miles down the road, he swung onto Blackbird Boulevard. The Twin Bears was on the edge of town, well away from the upscale shops and restaurants. It had a big parking lot with wide spaces to accommodate pickup trucks and family-friendly SUVs.

Gina recombed and refastened her ponytail before they left the vehicle.

They crossed the lot to a covered porch and a set of wide wood-beamed doors that were the main entrance. He grasped the oversize handle to pull the door open and let Gina go in first.

The Twin Bears was a lively place with a big square bar in the center that had seating all around it. Polished wood tables with rounded burgundy leather chairs were nicely spaced throughout the rest of the big dining room. Two of the walls were dotted with windows, showcasing miniature palm tree gardens with little white lights that were just coming on in the dusk.

It was a seat yourself kind of place, and Rafe led them to a table against a brick feature wall.

A waitress immediately appeared to fill two red-tinted water glasses with a stream of ice water.

"Can I get y'all something to drink?" she asked.

Rafe looked to Gina.

"What should I try?" she surprised him by asking.

"I'm getting an Irish Freeze. It's a coffee, caramel, whiskey milkshake."

"Our most popular," the young waitress said. She handed Gina a slim drink menu. "But we've got Guinness and Baileys, peach bourbon, coconut chocolate rum, and boozy banana cream."

"Think I'll go with the favorite," Gina said with a

smile and handed back the menu. "When in Rome." Her gaze turned to Rafe and went warm.

Which had him thinking about their kiss again.

The waitress handed them each a food menu and disappeared.

"Do I even need to look at this?" Gina asked him. "Or can I count on your expertise?"

"I'm getting a loaded Angus burger with wedge fries—messy sauce, but well worth it."

She didn't hesitate. "You haven't led me wrong so far today."

"You're having an Angus burger?" He couldn't hide his surprise.

She hadn't struck him as a messy burger kind of woman. Then again, she hadn't stuck him as a milkshake kind of gal, either. She was slender and, well, to be blunt, pretty fussy. He'd have expected her to look for a kale and responsibly harvested seafood salad.

"Sure," she said, a challenge in her expression.

"Is this the clothes?" he asked with a thread of humor. "Did they magically change Gina Edmond from a princess to a cowgirl?"

"This princess has a lot of layers to her."

The waitress arrived with their drinks, and Rafe placed their dinner order. Afterward, Gina took a sip of her milkshake, and her eyes went wide.

"Good?" he asked.

"*Amazing.* I don't usually indulge in things like this."

"Imagine my surprise."

"Hey."

"I took you for a cabernet sauvignon hundred-point grand cru kind of woman."

"Now you're just baiting me," she accused.

"A little," he admitted. "But tell me it's not true. Tell me your daddy's wine cellar isn't full of old-world wines from the very best years of overpriced vineyards."

"I wouldn't know."

"Not a wine person?" That surprised him.

"I drink whatever the chef pours."

Rafe couldn't help but laugh. "The was the snobbiest defense of snobbery I've ever heard."

"I meant I don't spend any time in *Daddy's* wine cellar."

"I know. But you have to admit…"

She took another sip of her milkshake. "I don't have to admit anything to you. I think you have wine envy."

"Me?" He hated that it came out like a weak question instead of a strong denial. He hated it more that she was right. He'd kill for Rusty Edmond's wine cellar.

"No restaurant can compete with a private collection," she allowed. "Unless you've got nothing but millionaires as your clientele."

"We've been increasing and improving our selection."

She looked guilty. "I shouldn't have picked on you."

Great. Now he had her pity. How had *that* happened?

"I have plenty of fine wines at RCW."

"And I have a terrific milkshake." She stirred it with her straw.

Their burgers arrived then, hot and fragrant on huge wooden platters.

She looked the half-pound monstrosity up and down. It was layered with tomatoes, lettuce, mushrooms and Twin Bears' famous sauce.

Rafe could see she was overwhelmed.

He lifted the sharp wood-handled knife from his cutlery selection. "Want me to cut it in half for you?"

"Yes, please."

He reached across the table and sliced through her burger.

"I don't depend on my dad for everything," she said as she wrapped a paper napkin over the rounded edge of a burger half.

"Who said you did?"

"You implied it."

He lifted his burger from the sides, knowing the sauce would drip onto his plate. "You're the precious daughter of a town legend. Everybody thinks you've had an easy ride."

"In some ways I suppose I have," she agreed.

"Current situation notwithstanding," Rafe concurred. "But even with the embezzlement, your family's in better shape than most." He took a first bite of the juicy burger. It was as delicious as he'd remembered.

"And I'm trying to do my part to help the town."

Rafe nodded his agreement with that.

Gina took a first bite. Like she had with the milkshake, her eyes lit up with appreciation. "Mmm."

"Right? And you don't even have to dress up for it." He looked around at the other patrons, all casually dressed, many of them families. And then turned to take in the cheerful waitstaff moving efficiently from table to table amid the hum of friendly conversation.

"It's a nice place," Gina agreed. "Laid-back, relaxed."

"You don't do this often?" Rafe couldn't help but ask.

"Eat hamburgers?"

"Relax."

The question seemed to stump her. "How do you mean?"

"Take time for yourself...enjoy some peace and quiet, a little comfort food, maybe read a book."

"You do know where I live, right?" It was a rhetorical question.

He answered anyway. "The infamous Elegance Ranch."

"Not exactly a hotbed of casual peace and quiet," she told him, taking another draw on her milkshake. "Wow. This is sinfully tasty."

He thought about warning her that it packed a punch but decided against it. At the same time, he flagged the waitress for a cup of coffee so he could switch to a non-alcoholic beverage. "No privacy?" he prompted her.

"CEOs of major oil companies don't punch out at five o'clock."

"You're not a CEO of a major oil company."

"I live with one, and I work for one."

"It bleeds into your homelife?"

"It's no secret that my dad isn't one for big social gatherings. But he does his share of schmoozing."

"You'd have to at his level," Rafe reasoned. He himself made sure to stay in touch with industry organizations and his fellow restaurateurs, also with suppliers and marketing influencers.

Locking eyes with him, she took another drink. She'd made it about halfway through her burger and eaten quite a few of the fries.

He was surprised she'd done that well, given the size of the meal and the size of her. "Can I ask you something?"

"Go for it." She picked up another crispy fry. "These things are addictive."

"What do you do in the evenings when your father is entertaining business associates?"

"Smile," she said.

"And?"

"Nod. I nod a lot."

"I thought you had a job with the company."

"I do."

"What's your title?"

She hesitated a moment before answering. "Senior vice president of corporate relations."

"Relations with who?"

Her lighthearted mood abruptly disappeared. "Are you done? Should we get going?"

Five

Gina might be on the move now, but it was hardly smooth sailing.

Mandee Meriweather and *Royal Tonight!* were now on board for the auction, and Gina had thirty-two cowboys signed up—since two more had called after the recruitment drive. She also had her full project plan mapped out on her laptop. But she had a long way to go on plan implementation, and a very tough sales pitch to make to her father.

As she entered the reception hall of the Elegance Ranch, with its cool marble floor and twin curving wrought iron staircases leading to the second floor, she could hear her father's voice from the library through the carved wooden archway. She hoped whoever was with him this evening wouldn't stay long. Their conversation was going to be difficult, and she wanted to get it over with.

"That is *not* what I wanted to hear," her father complained.

Great. He was in a mood. Then again, when wasn't he in a mood lately?

Nobody answered, but that didn't stop him from continuing. "He didn't just disappear into thin air. Can we not get the FBI involved?" Rusty went silent for a minute. "That's what I'm paying you *top* dollar for. To get me results."

Gina guessed he was on the phone, presumably talking to the private investigation firm he'd hired to look for Billy. Rusty wasn't ready to admit Billy was his son from a long-ago affair with Antoinette Holmes. But Billy's social media posts were getting increasingly darker.

He claimed to have become Ross's college roommate and confidant to use what he learned about the Edmond family to worm his way in. It was a revenge plot years in the making and a thousand lies in its execution, and Gina felt sick every time she discovered something new.

She considered going up to her room and talking to her father later. But she'd steeled herself for this conversation, and she wanted to get it over with. She dropped her purse on a side table and waited for the phone call to end.

"See that you do," Rusty all but shouted into the phone. "I'll be waiting on an answer."

Silence reigned until the library's grandfather clocked bonged the hour. Gina waited a minute longer before walking briskly into the richly furnished wood-paneled room to find her father standing in front of the main bookshelf, next to the spotless cherrywood desk.

"Hello, Dad."

"You're home." He seemed surprised to see her and not particularly happy.

She didn't seek him out often these days. Not that he'd ever been her favorite conversational partner or had ever paid much attention to her one way or the other.

"There's something I'd like to talk to you about," she said.

His gaze narrowed. "I don't need any more bad news."

"It's not bad news. It's good news." She plowed forward before he had a chance to react. "Ross told you we were planning a fundraising auction for the business community?"

Rusty frowned at her. "He certainly told me you'd pledged Edmond money for it."

"Some," she said. "The three of us all agreed."

"I don't remember agreeing."

"Dad."

"Don't *Dad* me."

"Billy was—"

"*Not* my son, that's what Billy is," her father snapped.

"Billy was our responsibility."

"And how do you figure that?"

Gina realized she'd made a tactical error. Talk of Billy was only going to infuriate her father.

She quickly backtracked. "I wanted to talk some more about the auction."

His glare would ordinarily have stopped her.

"Yes, we pledged some family money," she continued. "And it was the right thing to do. The Edmond family has always been a huge part of the local business community. I was always told, by you, that we prided ourselves on our participation. As far back as I can remember, you said we were pivotal to the success of the town."

He waved a dismissive hand, but he didn't outright disagree.

"The auction is a good idea. Lots of people are buying in. Thirty-two cowboys have stepped up, and *Royal Tonight!* is going to broadcast the program. Mandee Meriweather has even agreed to host." Gina could tell she had her father's interest.

Mandee was flamboyant and attention-seeking, but Gina always had the impression her father admired the on-air host. She'd assumed it was because the woman could be influential. The three things Rusty admired most were money, power and influence.

"We expect to make good money on it," Gina said. "But we need a location for the live broadcast."

"They have a studio."

"That's way too small and not nearly enough pizzazz."

"Pizzazz?"

"We need thousands, tens of thousands of people to tune in to watch the broadcast and log in online. We need an interesting location, a magnificent location to help draw them in."

"Did you have a specific place in mind?"

"Yes," she murmured.

"And where would that be?"

"The Elegance Ranch."

Her father stared at her, looking more perplexed than angry. But then her meaning seemed to sink in. *"What!?"*

The force of his question nearly made her step back.

"Have you lost your mind?" he demanded.

She stood her ground. "It would be perfect. We could

use the back patio, the lawn for seating, the pool gaze-
bos as a balancing feature…"

"No! Absolutely not. TV cameras? In the house?
What are you even *thinking*?"

The reaction was pretty much what Gina had expected, but she wasn't done yet. "It's not like we'd film
in your bedroom."

Rusty's mouth moved, but no sounds came out. At
the same time, his face turned a comical red color.

"And it's not as if the family secrets are just lying out
there on the coffee tables for anyone to see," she said.

He found his voice. "We don't have secrets."

"Great. Then there's no reason not to let the world
see a little bit of life behind the scenes." She made a
small space between her thumb and forefinger. "Just a
little bit of our magnificent house."

"No."

"It's for a good cause."

"Do it at the Cattleman's Club."

"Nobody's going to tune in to see the Cattleman's
Club, but the Elegance Ranch…now that would be an
audience draw."

"Ghoulish curiosity," Rusty said with disgust.

"Take away a little of the mystery," she said. "Show
them we're a normal, functional, happy family."

He tilted his head in obvious incomprehension.

"We can pull it off," she cajoled. "People will be too
busy looking at the furniture, the sculptures and the
paintings to pay much attention to the people. And if
we show them the wine cellar?"

"The *wine* cellar?"

"Okay, maybe not the wine cellar. It's so big, we'd
look like we overindulged in liquor every night. But

the reception hall, the great room, the patio and yard, and here." She gestured around the library. "The most personal we'd get is the kitchen and dining room. It'll make us look more ordinary. It might tone down some of the gossip."

He didn't respond for a minute, and she grew hopeful. Had her reasoning worked on him? "Just think about it."

"Where did you even come up with such an asinine—"

"Dad?" Ross appeared in the archway.

The tension remained between father and son, but it was diminishing as the weeks went past.

Ross glanced between Gina and Rusty, taking in their posture and expressions. "What's going on?"

Rusty rounded on his son. "Will you talk some sense into your sister?"

Ross looked to Gina.

"I'm asking about holding the auction here," she said.

Comprehension came into his eyes.

Gina put a pleading look into her own. She needed her brother's support on this. "We have everyone on board. It's going to work, Ross. I *know* it is. We just have to have a stellar location to bring it all together."

"Elegance Ranch is not some tacky Hollywood film location," Rusty groused.

Gina bit her tongue. "We need a big audience," she said, spreading her arms wide. "The bigger the better. That's how we get the bidding up high. That's how we make real money. That's how we save Royal businesses."

"But does it have to be here?" Ross asked. "Surely another venue besides our family home can—"

"No!" Gina cut in. "No. I don't ask for much around here. I show up when the rest of you need me. I smile. I nod. I don't push my ideas in the company. Even when I think of something—even when I see opportunities— I keep my mouth shut because that seems to be the way everyone wants it. But *I* want this. I *need* this. This is *my* project, and last time I checked, this was my house, too."

She stopped talking, and the room went dead silent.

The grandfather clock chimed the quarter hour, a single bong. It seemed significant somehow.

Ross stared at her as if he couldn't believe what he'd just heard.

She couldn't really believe it, either. Confrontation was not her strong suit.

Rusty cleared his throat. "Well. You sounded a little bit like your mother there."

Gina didn't imagine that could be good. She tensed, waiting for him to reject her idea again, wondering if she should argue back one more time or simply give up and accept inevitable defeat.

"I suppose if you stuck to the main floor," her father said.

It took Gina a moment to absorb what she'd heard. Even then, she didn't quite believe it. "So...*yes*?"

Rusty nodded, but he also frowned. "But I don't want to be tripping over these people. You hear me?"

"Loud and clear. We'll stick to one day, maybe two if they need some setup time." She hoped she wasn't making a promise she couldn't keep.

"I can always take a drive down to Mustang Point," Rusty grumbled. "Got some things to do there anyway."

It was all Gina could do not to cheer out loud. She couldn't wait to call Lila and give her the good news.

It was Sunday, so Rafe's mother, Carmen, was happily bustling around the yard of the ranch house making sure everyone at the cookout had a drink and was sampling her grilled peppers and empanadas. The family was all here—Rafe's father and grandfather, Lorenzo and Valencia, along with Matias who was entertaining the ranch hands' kids by throwing a lasso, plus Rafe's two younger brothers, Tomas and Diego. About twenty assorted hands and staff members from the Cortez-Williams Ranch were also in attendance. Diego was currently strumming his guitar for a small appreciative audience.

The only person who looked happier than Carmen was Gina, and Rafe settled back to watch her from a distance. He was gratified to see her again after their dinner at the Twin Bears had ended so disappointingly. He took responsibility for that, for letting the conversation go in a negative direction. He liked teasing her too much, and he'd ended up annoying her.

She was working with a photographer now at his family ranch. Apparently she'd decided the fun of the cookout would make a nice addition to the auction website photo array. The photographer had taken landscapes this morning and was focused on Matias and his lasso right now.

Rafe figured his turn would come next. He wasn't crazy about being a model for the website advertising, but he'd suck it up and let them take a few shots of him dressed in blue jeans and a Stetson, especially if it gave him a chance to spend more time with Gina.

Her mood had soured so abruptly at the Twin Bears that he hadn't found a way to work the conversation back around to the kiss. He felt like she owed him one, or he owed *her* one, assuming she was still willing.

He watched from a distance, thinking she hadn't exactly dressed the part of cowgirl today. Her black pants were snug to the ankles, showing off her toned legs. She wore a white tank top layered under a filmy sapphire blouse that flashed bright in the sunshine. Her heels were low, but her boots were a pale cream color, a risk on a ranch for sure. She also wore a gold pendant necklace, a matching bracelet that jangled enough to scare a horse, and a pair of long earrings below a messy knot of hair up high on the top of her head.

He was also thinking she was stunningly beautiful, and he couldn't stop staring at her, remembering their dinner, her expressions and gestures, how much she'd loved the milkshake and how he'd wished they were on a real date. He *needed* to find a new reason to kiss her. And quick. Because she looked absolutely ravishing in the late-afternoon sun.

His mother approached Gina, clearly offering her an empanada. Gina tried to say no, but Rafe knew that was a losing proposition. His mother had raised five boys on a working ranch. In her mind, there was no such thing as being too full since you'd likely burn off the excess calories in the following twenty minutes.

Carmen's determination worked yet again, and Rafe smiled to himself as Gina accepted one of the little empanadas. She took a bite, and her eyes went wide. He guessed it was spicier than she'd anticipated. But she smiled and nodded, obviously telling his mom it was delicious.

But when Carmen turned away, Gina wiped her eyes with the back of her hand.

Rafe took pity on her and started across the lawn, weaving his way through groups of people who were laughing and drinking punch, past the five picnic tables and around the grill where his dad, Lorenzo Jr., was grilling under a billow of smoke and surrounded by the tasty aroma of beef.

"What'll you take on your burger?" his dad asked as he drew close.

"In a minute, Papa."

"What do you mean *in a minute*? They're ready now."

"The works, then," he said over his shoulder. "I'll be right back." A few steps later, he was beside Gina.

"Hi," he said.

She looked up from cautiously eyeing the empanada. "Oh, hi."

He couldn't help but smile at the flush in her cheeks.

He leaned close. "When I say…"

"When you say what?"

"When I say *now*, hand it over."

She looked confused. "Hand what over?"

"The empanada. My mom makes the best ones in three counties, but you need to work up a tolerance for the habaneros."

A wave of relief crossed Gina's face as she glanced around and lowered her voice. "I don't think I've done that yet."

"Now," he said, seeing his mother's back was turned.

Gina surreptitiously handed it over, and he popped it into his mouth.

"Thanks," she said. "You saved me."

"No hardship. I love these things."

"I'm impressed with the strength of your palate."

Rafe didn't recognize the photographer taking the unscripted shots of Matias and wondered if he was associated with *Royal Tonight!* "Who's that guy?"

"Quentin Waters," Gina said. "He's part of our marketing department."

"At the Edmond Organization?"

Gina nodded.

"You got Rusty on board?" Rafe was surprised by that. He'd taken the oil tycoon's absence from the Chamber of Commerce meeting to mean he'd wanted nothing to do with the fundraising effort.

"I wouldn't exactly say *on board*. But he did agree to us hosting the auction at Elegance Ranch."

That shocked Rafe even more. "How'd you ever pull that off?"

"Smiled and batted my princess eyelashes."

"Daddy's little girl?"

"That was sarcasm, Rafe."

"Oh." He'd taken her literally, earning himself an irritated frown.

She continued with exaggerated patience. "If you must know, I explained the merits of a compelling location in growing the audience size and therefore forcing the bidding higher so more Royal businesses could benefit from the funding raised."

Rafe felt bad for making the quip. "That sounds very logical."

"I wish you wouldn't sound so surprised that I'm logical."

"I'm not surprised." He wasn't, exactly. It simply hadn't occurred to him that logic and reason would be her go-to strategy for persuading her father.

"Rafe?" his own father called out from behind him.

"You want a burger?" He was more than happy to change the subject.

She shook her head. "I'm working. I don't expect your family to feed me."

"Don't let the spicy empanada scare you. The burgers are quite tame." He called out to the photographer. "Hey, Quentin. Come and get a burger. Matias, bring the man along and feed him." To Gina, he said, "When in Rome, remember?"

She capitulated with a look of surrender, and Rafe squelched an urge to take her hand.

After collecting their burgers, they got settled at one end of a picnic table, Rafe and Gina across from Matias and Quentin.

"Turn sideways," Quentin said to Rafe.

Rafe swallowed and did as the other man asked. "Why?" He didn't see anything untoward, just a bunch of kids climbing a fence and a couple of dogs rushing around beneath them.

"I want to check out your profile," Quentin said.

Rafe used it as an excuse to turn Gina's way.

She turned to meet his gaze.

He'd thought all this time that her eyes were rich mocha, bordering on hazel. But he'd been wrong. In the sunlight he could see they were much more complex, with spikes of green radiating from the pupils and a blue-gray ring at the edge of the iris. They were exotically beautiful. He'd never seen anything quite like them.

He was about to say something when Quentin interrupted.

"Little more," the photographer said.

Rafe didn't want to move. He wanted to stay right here in this position and stare into Gina's eyes forever.

"Toward the back," Quentin instructed.

Rafe moved his head but kept looking at Gina.

Her expression smoothed out, and her lips seemed to soften as she gazed back.

"With a Stetson," Quentin said. "Can you see it?"

Rafe realized the man was talking to Matias.

"See what?" Matias asked. "Rafe's ugly mug?" He took a bite of his burger.

Gina's face broke into an amused smile.

"At sunset," Quentin said. "Maybe leaning on a fence post, that profile, hat pulled down, little bend to the head. Oh, yeah. We gotta get that."

Matias was staring openly at Quentin now, clearly confounded by his level of enthusiasm.

For that matter, so was Rafe. "I'm not—"

"He's saying you'll look rugged," Gina said. "Outdoorsy, über cowboy."

Matias made a sound of disgust. "I'm more cowboy than he is. I ride bucking horses. Heck, I breed bucking horses. Rafe waits snooty tables."

Rafe chuckled while Gina turned back his way, looking shocked that Matias would insult him and clearly bracing herself for his reaction.

"I do wait tables sometimes," Rafe said easily. "And Matias means he used to ride broncs when he was young and fit."

This time his brother grinned at the comeback.

Gina looked equally worried, like the good-natured ribbing might turn into an actual fight.

"Relax," Rafe told her. "We're just joking around."

"I know just the spot," Quentin broke in, his mind

obviously firmly on his photography. "The split-rail fence beside that old windmill where the river bends into the shallows. We can get those oak trees in the background. But we have to hurry."

Rafe checked the sky and agreed they had to hurry if they wanted to catch the sunset. It was a twenty-minute drive then a fifteen-minute walk to the old windmill—and that wasn't even accounting for Gina's fashion boots.

He couldn't say he was happy about Quentin going all artistic-vision on this, but mostly he wanted to get it over with. So he dug into his burger, and soon they were all traipsing into a pickup truck.

When Matias started to hop into the pickup box, Rafe handed him the keys and told him to drive. Before Matias could ask why, Rafe ushered Quentin into the middle of the bench seat, then Rafe climbed in and gestured for Gina to sit on his knee. It was an obvious trick, and he could tell by the amused expression on his brother's face that he knew exactly what Rafe was doing. But Rafe didn't care.

Gina hesitated for a second, but then gamely climbed in.

He shut the door and left his arm circled around her.

Matias was a speedy driver, leaving Gina with little choice but to brace herself against Rafe's shoulder as they skimmed along the gravel road. He loved the feel of her in his lap, her soft buttocks and firm thighs pressing down on his, her warm shoulder tucked against his, and the side of her breast just grazing his chest.

Arm on the rest, he let his fingertips brush the side of her thigh. Her pants were thin and taut, and he imagined he could feel the satin of her skin beneath the fabric. Loose wisps of her hair fanned his cheek, and he inhaled the light citrus scent, thinking he'd never look at oranges the same way again.

Matias rocked the truck to a stop at the trailhead, and Rafe opened the passenger-side door. He was gratified when Gina didn't jump straight out. She seemed to take a little time, accepting the arm he offered and slipping down to the ground.

The path to the old windmill was wide and scenic as it wound toward the river.

Gina was keeping up, even though her boots seemed far from ideal for the dusty walk.

"That's the spot," Quentin said as they came out on the flat grassy meadow.

He felt like a prize heifer being posed for a money shot. But then Gina smiled encouragingly, and he thought about the return trip with her on his lap.

"Put on the hat and lean your elbow on the post," Quentin instructed, lining up his camera and adjusting his position. "Now look to the south. This light is amazing. Magic hour."

The photographer had Rafe move around for a dozen more shots.

"What are you going to do with all these pictures?" he asked Gina once he was finished.

"A montage for each of you. I've got the tech team at Edmond putting together the website."

"Whatever works." He loved watching her face in the soft light, listening to her sweet voice.

"We'll also do a behind-the-scenes house tour as a teaser and an opener to the program."

"Rusty agreed to that?"

"I figure it counts as part of the auction."

"I'm not the one you have to convince."

She frowned at that. "But you think it's a good idea, right?"

Given the chance, Rafe would watch a video on where Gina lived—too bad it wouldn't include her bedroom.

He pictured her surrounded by pastels and florals, stretched out on a queen-size bed, dressed in silk and satin, or maybe lace. His fingers twitched with the need to touch her, and he subconsciously moved closer still.

A breeze blew the strands of her hair over her pink cheeks. His gaze dropped to her full lips, and he suddenly realized the silence had stretched between them. She was waiting for him to react. Too bad he couldn't remember what she'd said.

Matias's and Quentin's voices grew more distant as they worked their way along the riverbank.

"I'm impressed," Rafe answered, meaning it on a whole bunch of levels.

"It's really coming together."

The breeze picked up again, and her hair fluttered across her face. Without thinking, he brushed it back. His fingertips fanned her cheek, and they both stilled.

"I still want to kiss you." He said the thing that was most on his mind, easing closer. "We got sidetracked the other night."

Her gaze flickered to Matias and Quentin beside the river. "That's a bad idea."

Rafe glanced over his shoulder. "They're not paying any attention."

"We're out in the open."

He crossed the final inches between them. "That seems kind of exciting to me."

"Rafe." She put her palm to his chest.

"What? Don't tell me no, Princess. It's just a kiss."

She glanced worriedly over her shoulder again. But then she looked back. "Make it quick."

Rafe wasn't sure he could comply with that directive, but he was willing to do his best. He touched her chin, tipping it gently toward him while he shifted to block her from Matias's and Quentin's accidental view. Then he bent his head and brought his lips to hers. A wave of sweet tenderness bloomed between them. Driven by instinct, he firmed the kiss, parting his lips. His hand splayed into her hair while the other moved to the small of her back and drew her closer, pressing her tight against the apex of his thighs.

His mind screamed at him to do more, bring her fully into his arms, deepen the kiss, make it long and thorough, then kiss her over and over and over again.

A small moan vibrated from her lips, and her hands squeezed down on his shoulders.

He was struggling on the ragged edge of control.

"I don't *think so*," Matias called out.

Rafe jerked away.

Matias laughed, but when Rafe checked he was laughing at something Quentin had said. Neither of them had looked this way.

"Sorry," Rafe rasped, turning back to Gina. "They didn't see."

Her cheeks were fully flushed now, and her lips were deep red. Her eyes seemed to glow with an inner desire. "We can't."

"We didn't." At least they hadn't done anything that was anywhere near what Rafe had wanted to do.

Out of desperation, he forced an air of nonchalance. "It was nothing, just a simple kiss."

Six

After their explosive kiss, Gina avoided Rafe in the days leading up to the auction. It might have been nothing to him, but that "simple" kiss had rocked her world.

She'd been kissed in the past, had prior romances. Which amounted to fleeting relationships compared to most of her friends. She'd never been head over heels about a man, and maybe that's why her kissing track record was so lackluster. But not anymore. Rafe's lip-lock had shown her what was possible. It was embarrassing to admit how badly she wanted to do it again.

Luckily, she was busy, the busiest she'd ever been, taking care of the auction details. She was also energized by the work. It felt good to matter, to have what she did be important to other people.

All that effort was coming together on the morning of the auction. She was nervous, hadn't slept much the night before and got up early to run through the last-minute details. Now she was hovering in the entrance hall waiting for Mandee Meriweather to arrive for the behind-the-scenes house tour.

As he'd sworn he would, her father had left for Mustang Point yesterday as soon as the first technical crews showed up.

Today was a split-second operation. Mandee and the crew would film the tour of the main floor, then the cooking staff would start putting together all the fancy hors d'oeuvres they would serve to the in-person guests. The gardeners were setting out white folding chairs in perfect rows on the lawn between the pool and the back terrace that would serve as the stage.

For now, three SUVs drove into the roundabout, stopping at the front of the house. Gina opened the double doors wide to welcome Mandee, her director, Sebastian, and the film crew.

"Good morning," she called out cheerfully as they all trooped inside, equipment in hand as they fanned out across the marble floor of the hall.

Mandee removed her sunglasses and looked around with interest.

"Let's start out in here," she said to Sebastian, before sparing Gina a quick glance. "Hi, Gina."

Over the past two weeks, she had found the celebrity reporter to be both brusque and demanding. She was the queen of her domain and assumed everyone existed to cater to her whims. Watching Mandee's behavior, Gina couldn't help thinking about Rafe telling her she was a princess. She hoped her attitude was better than Mandee's and hated to think she came across as that entitled.

"Sweep through the front door." Mandee continued

barking out orders to Sebastian. "And get a panoramic of the staircase. After that, just follow along."

"You heard Mandee," he said to the camera crew. "We'll upload footage on the fly to the editor's suite. We're on a deadline, people."

Everyone started to move as if it were a choreographed play.

Gina quickly stepped out of the way.

They followed Mandee from polished wood-paneled rooms to artwork-accented spaces as she exclaimed over the paintings, sculptures and furnishings. They paused in the rotunda, then again in the dining room with Mandee asking viewers to imagine themselves being invited to a lavish party at the Elegance Ranch. Then they stopped in the kitchen, taking note of the blue labradorite countertops before the cameras scanned to the family room where Mandee unexpectedly asked Gina what it was like to grow up in the mansion.

Caught off guard, she didn't want to sound like a spoiled princess in her castle. "I liked the stable best," she said on a little laugh. "Between the horses and the pool, it was hard to get me inside the house."

"Most kids make do with a front yard and a sprinkler," Mandee said. There was an edge to her voice that brought Gina's hackles up.

"Royal has some of the best junior horse riders in the state," Gina added, ignoring the jab. "And most of the cowboys in tonight's auction grew up on horseback right here in Maverick and Colonial Counties."

Mandee looked annoyed by the deflection, but she broadened her smile.

"On that note," she said into the closest camera, "please stay tuned to this special broadcast of *Royal*

Tonight! and enjoy this exclusive invitation onto the Elegance Ranch. Better still, make a bid in the auction and come on out to visit us in person here in Royal, Texas."

"Cut!" Sebastian called out. Then he made a whirling motion. "Let's grab some B-roll to flesh it out."

The crew started to film various angles of the family room and the kitchen.

"Main floor only," Gina reminded them. The last thing she needed was to run afoul of her father.

"Where's my greenroom?" the TV host asked to no one in particular.

Sebastian looked to Gina. "Where can Mandee rest and freshen up?"

Gina quickly improvised. "Donna?" she called to the head housekeeper, who she knew was hovering off the kitchen waiting for the camera crews to finish.

Donna quickly appeared. "How can I help?"

"Can you show Mandee to the guesthouse?" To Sebastian, she said, "It's nice and private."

Nobody had used the guesthouse since Billy had so unceremoniously hightailed it out of Royal. On Rusty's orders, it had been cleaned top to bottom to erase any sign of his stay. It had two self-contained bedroom suites in case Queen Mandee needed a nap or a shower.

"Please follow me." Donna gestured the way toward a door to the back veranda.

"I'll have some refreshments sent over," Gina told Mandee as she left.

Several members of the cooking staff made their appearance as the camera crew finally trailed out of the kitchen, clearing the way.

When the last crew member left, Gina grinned at Horatio, the mansion's head chef. "It's go time!"

* * *

If Rafe had known then what he knew now, he never would have volunteered for the cowboy experience auction. Ever since his auction listing had gone up on the website, he'd been inundated with both questions and *questionable* offers. Some were about the ranch and the experience, but more were about him personally.

Quentin should have made clear what he was doing with that sunset profile photo. It had sounded innocuous enough at the time—make Rafe look like a rugged old-time cowboy who knew his way around horses and cattle. And sure, that made sense for the sake of the auction.

But what Quentin *hadn't* said was that he'd planned to make Rafe look like some Hollywood version of a cowboy. The filtered sunset, the tilt of his head, the warm light reflecting off his chin… It was all too much. At first, Rafe had accused Quentin of retouching the picture, misleading anyone who'd be bidding on his experience. But Quentin had sworn he hadn't retouched a thing.

Rafe had then tried to get him to take it down and replace it with something less personal, but the website marketing team gave him a flat-out no. And since Rafe hadn't set any restrictions on how they could use the photos, he couldn't convince them to change it. They'd also told him his listing was garnering more interest than any of the other cowboys'. Matias was a close second, and Tucker McCoy was a surprising third.

He walked through the open doors of the Edmond mansion. When he spotted Gina from afar, he admitted he'd do it all over again. To get up close and personal with her, especially to hold her in his arms and share that mind-blowing kiss beside the windmill, it was worth it.

"Champagne?" a formally dressed waiter asked him.

"No, thanks." Rafe wasn't in the mood for anything sweet and bubbly.

"If you'd prefer something else, there's a full bar service available beside the pool."

"Thanks," Rafe said, taking in the well-dressed crowd, feeling out of place in his gray-and-blue-plaid shirt, worn blue jeans and wide leather belt. He'd shaved, trimmed his hair and ironed the shirt, but he'd been forced to wear a pair of scuffed cowboy boots. All he had were the ones he'd worn while working on the ranch, and every pair had seen a whole lot of miles. But he'd promised Gina he'd come dressed like a cowboy.

Right now, he looked for a place to ditch his Stetson until the bidding started. There was an open room next to him in the entry hall, so he took a look inside. It was a library, and he found a desk in a corner to set his hat. When he turned, Gina was coming in through the archway.

"Oh, it's you," she said. "Glad you're on time."

A shaft of warmth pierced his chest, and he sucked in a tight breath as she came closer.

She looked sexy and sophisticated, hair up, makeup fresh and bright. Her dress was fitted flat lace, both structured and soft at the same time. The blazer gave her a no-nonsense air, while her pretty sandals accentuated her amazing legs.

"I'm punctual," he said for something to add to the conversation. What he really wanted to say was she was beautiful and could they please get out of here and go someplace private.

"Did you get some champagne?" she asked in full-on hostess mode. She came to a halt a couple feet away.

"I'm not crazy about champagne," he admitted.

"Something else then? A beer?" A sparkle came into her eyes. "I didn't think to plan for milkshakes."

He smiled at that. He liked that she referenced their dinner together. It felt like an in-joke, like they were more of a thing than they actually were. They weren't even close to being a thing. But he'd like it if they were. What guy wouldn't?

"I'm good," he said, easing as close as he dared.

"You should go mix and mingle a bit. It could bring up the bids from the local crowd. We had three hundred people register as in-person bidders." She leaned in and lowered her voice. "But I think there are some crashers here."

His hands twitched with the need to touch her. "They probably want to check out your mansion." He looked around the library. "Spectacular place you've got here."

Gina gave a cursory glance to the bookshelves, the opulent furniture, the rich rug and the chevron hardwood floor that on its own must have cost a fortune. "I can't take any credit. I didn't even decorate my own bedroom."

Rafe once again tried to picture her bedroom. "Is it like this room?" he asked.

"You know, Mandee asked me earlier what it was like to grow up here. I didn't have an answer for her."

Rafe squelched his disappointment at not getting any bedroom details. "Do you have an answer now?"

"Not really." Gina looked like she was thinking hard. "Maybe. Truth is, it was surreal, like I didn't have a real home. I had a place where I slept and where I ate, but other people decorated and cleaned them, other folks planned and cooked the meals. My clothes and toys simply appeared. I never needed to want anything. I never had time."

The Cortez-Williamses owned a big spread and had wealth and power in their own right, but they'd worked their tails off for every scrap of it, every generation from his three-times-great-grandfather to him and his brothers, and the next generation would do the same. The family money didn't go into children's toys, it went into buildings and equipment, feed and vet care, wages for the ranch hands and workers.

"I've done chores since I was seven years old." He gave a small chuckle of remembrance. "Probably before that, too, although I wouldn't have been much help."

"What kind of chores?"

"Typical ranch stuff—feeding the chickens, gathering eggs, mucking out the barn. It's a never-ending cycle of feed and manure."

Her expression turned thoughtful again. "I rode the horses, never fed them, though. Well, a handful of oats or a carrot as a treat after riding, but a little girl wouldn't have been trusted to manage the hay and water."

"Tossing out vegetable scraps for the chickens isn't exactly a complex undertaking. I didn't have any sisters, so I don't know what girls would have done growing up. Baking bread, maybe."

"Wow. That was sexist."

He shrugged. "I only know my own experience. My mom and nana loved the kitchen, and my dad and grandfather spend their lives outdoors. But I suppose you could have made a case for shoveling manure along with the rest of us."

"Didn't ever do that either," she looked embarrassed to admit.

"What did you do besides riding?" He was curious now about her life growing up.

"Piano, gymnastics, dance."

"You took dancing lessons?" He pictured himself dancing with her in a fancy ballroom, an orchestra playing. She'd look stunning in his arms.

"A little ballet, modern dance, ballroom. I needed to hold my own at parties."

"Ahhh, the parties. Couldn't have those go bad on you," he teased.

"They were business functions mostly. And those dancing skills come in handy to this day."

"I suppose they would."

She quirked a brow. "Are you saying you don't dance?"

"Sure, I dance. But we did it for fun, no lessons. Papa and Diego play guitar, and everyone in the family would sing or dance. Some Saturday nights, everyone who worked on the ranch would be out on the patio whooping it up."

"That sounds like fun."

"It was fun, lots of fun." There were times when Rafe missed the close-knit community he'd belonged to on the ranch, seeing his mother, father and his brothers every day, working alongside them and coming home at night with a sense of satisfaction along with the exhaustion.

"What is it?" Gina asked, peering closely at him.

"I was just remembering," he admitted.

"Remembering what?"

"My roots." Not that he wanted to delve into his dust-eating, manure-slinging roots with little miss ballet. He didn't expect her to understand the satisfaction of sweaty work or the simple pleasure of warm chocolate-cinnamon cookies on a Sunday evening.

"Different worlds," she said, sounding almost sad. Then she unexpectedly touched his cheek. "I'm picturing you as a young boy on a horse."

He willed her to keep her soft fingertips exactly where they were. "And I'm picturing you in a pink tutu."

She smiled at that. "I did have a pink one, frilly tulle and all."

He took a chance and eased forward. "You must have been delightful."

"That was my job back then." Her expression turned pensive. "Still my job now, mostly."

"But not today." He knew she'd worked hard on the auction.

She was so much more than just decorative on this project.

"That's nice of you to say." Her hand fell away from his face.

He captured it and shifted closer still. "It's the truth, Gina."

The noise from the get-together faded into the background. They were around a corner in the library, out of casual sight to people passing in the entry hall.

"I…" She seemed to run out of words.

Still holding her hand, he framed her smooth cheek with his rough palm. "You look wonderful today, professional, efficient, intelligent. Not to mention absolutely gorgeous."

He was rewarded with her sweet smile.

"You look rugged," she said, her voice dropping to a husky whisper. "Perfect...so sexy."

Want and desire and need all rose within him, simultaneously clamoring for him to take action.

She was here, right *here*, practically in his arms. She tipped her chin, slanting her lips, easing up enough to make it an invitation.

He took it, kissing her all over again, deeper this time, more amorously, as if his subconscious knew the way and had unleased his passion. He framed her face, then he wrapped his arms around her as the kiss went on and on.

She seemed more than willing, pressing against his thighs and his chest, rocketing his desire up notch after notch. She braced her hands on his shoulders as if he was her anchor.

In that moment, he *wanted* to be her anchor, her rock, the person she depended on for...he didn't even know what.

Too soon, voices sounded outside the room.

Rafe drew back, gazing with wonder into Gina's astonished eyes. Her lips were parted, swollen dark red with passion. Her cheeks were flushed again. Man, she was so incredibly beautiful.

He raised her hand to his lips and kissed the back of her fingers, drinking in the scent of her skin.

"Rafe?" she asked, a small tremble in her voice.

"This," he said, keeping her hand in his, her fingers still lightly brushing his lips, "is getting really hard to ignore."

She gave a wide-eyed nod of agreement.

"You going to be okay out there?" With a slant of his head, he gestured to the library entrance.

She looked that way, seeming to remember for the first time she had a major event going on outside these walls.

"Yes," she said, blinking to clear the passion from her eyes.

He immediately missed it.

But then she stepped back, and he released her hand, missing so much more than just the expression in her eyes.

She gave a hand gesture toward the entry. "I have to…uh…you know…"

"I know. Let's get me auctioned off."

It was standing room only on the back lawn. The three hundred white folding chairs that faced the terrace had quickly filled. Shade trees and the building's shadow helped offset the eighty-plus-degree heat.

Mandee was on the terrace now and anticipation was building as the first cowboy on the docket appeared off to one side.

Gina moved to the morning room where technical had been set up. Half the equipment was devoted to the *Royal Tonight!* broadcast, the other half dedicated to the social media interface. Ten people sat at makeshift desks with workstations or laptop computers, and the floor was a maze of wiring and computer towers. She stepped carefully around the cables.

"All systems go?" she asked Kane, Edmond's head of technology, coming up beside him where he was watching over tech Cassie Norio's shoulder.

"Analytics look fantastic. Good thing we added the surge capacity, or else we'd be crashing the website by now."

Gina realized she should leave him alone and let him work.

He gave her a nod and a wave as she headed outside to the opposite end of the terrace from the on-deck cowboy. The auction staging area was in the formal dining room on the other side of the house. They were being organized there by Lila and personally thanked by some notable members of the Royal Chamber of Commerce for their contributions to the cause.

Gina couldn't help picturing Rafe and wondering how she'd feel when he walked out for his turn. His kiss was still a tingle on her lips, and his embrace felt like it had left a permanent imprint on her body. Her mind wandered as the bidding got underway.

Pricing on the first cowboy went up quickly, and Mandee gaveled him off with a bang to get things started.

She introduced the second cowboy and started the bidding higher this time. People jumped in, and a jovial rivalry developed between the online bidders and the in-person audience. Every time a live person upped the bid over a virtual bidder, a large cheer came up from the crowd.

Gina's brother Ross appeared beside her. "Very well executed."

She took in the crowd again, the waiters still circulating with drinks and hors d'oeuvres. Mandee, whatever Gina might think of her personally, was doing a highly professional job as MC.

"Thanks," she said to Ross.

"Dad's still gone?"

"Last I saw. I doubt he'll be back before tomorrow."

"Probably a good thing," her brother said, looking

around. "He'd hate this. And someone would probably say something about Billy, and Dad would end up in an argument."

"Please, let's keep the drama to a minimum."

"So far, so good," he murmured.

Mandee brought the hammer down on the second cowboy. The experience went to an online bidder, and the crowd moaned in disappointment.

"They're really getting into this," Ross said on a chuckle. He took a sip of his champagne.

"Civic pride," Gina told him "But we want to sell as many experiences as possible outside Royal. We all agreed on that."

"The point being to bring in new money."

"Exactly," she replied. "Royal citizens are doing enough already. We need some Dallas or Chicago money, maybe LA or New York."

"You think big."

"I do," Gina answered with pride. She had thought big for this event, stretching and testing herself. She hoped she could find a way to keep doing that.

Tucker McCoy was up next, and he strutted out onto the terrace dressed in a bright red shirt, a leather vest with fringe and a pair of worn blue jeans covered in scuffed leather chaps. The online bidding turned fast and furious, with the bids mounting up at record speed.

The local audience seemed slightly stunned by the turn of events.

"I didn't expect that," Gina admitted.

"He's a character." Ross shook his head, taking another sip of his champagne. "You thirsty?"

She was. "I can go inside and grab something."

But her brother flagged down a waiter.

Tucker's experience went to an online bidder, setting a record by a wide margin.

While the cowboy held up his hands in victory, Ross handed Gina a glass of champagne.

She'd been avoiding alcohol as she managed the event. But then Rafe came out on the terrace to wait his turn, and she took a drink.

He took in the audience, then his attention went to Mandee.

Gina surreptitiously studied him, wondering how high his bids would go. What kind of women would like to spend a day with Rafe and—according to the outline on website—go horseback riding, move a cattle herd, meet foals and calves, and take a walk through the Cortez-Williams Ranch before enjoying a five-star steak dinner at RCW?

Gina, for one. She could easily picture herself doing all those things with Rafe.

Mandee enthusiastically called *sold* on the current cowboy, and Rafe walked across the makeshift stage. The crowd greeted him with energy and excitement, while Mandee gave him a glowing introduction.

Bids started from the crowd, and the internet quickly kicked in, the offers seeming to go up even faster than they had with Tucker.

"Well, I'm jumping in here myself," Mandee unexpectedly called out with glee, naming a number quite a bit higher than the last bid.

The move stunned Gina. "Can she do that?"

"She just did," Ross said on a laugh. "I guess if she's willing to shell out the cash…"

Gina didn't know the technicalities of formal auction rules, but Mandee jumping into the ring wasn't in the spirit of their overall plan.

"We all agreed we wanted sales from outside the city," Gina reminded Ross.

The bidding kept going up and up, and then Mandee called out another bid.

"This is *wild*," Ross said, sounding like he was having a jolly time.

Gina tried for another sip of champagne but discovered her glass was empty.

A local bidder upped the ante.

An online bidder came right back, then another, and another.

Mandee jumped in again.

Gina felt a surge of jealousy at the thought of the stunning TV host spending a full day with Rafe. Before she could think it through, she'd called out her own bid.

She could feel Ross's baffled gaze on her.

Mandee looked over her shoulder at Gina and frowned.

Gina didn't dare look at Rafe.

"I thought you wanted out-of-town bidders," he said.

"She's annoying me." Gina set her empty glass on a side table and glanced around for a waiter, thinking she could use another.

"Looks like your ploy worked," her brother remarked, nodding to the readout board as it displayed more incoming bids.

Gina hadn't intended to get the online bidders to go higher, but she pretended she had.

Some live audience members added to the bidding, then two people online duked it out for a few minutes, each going up in healthy increments.

Mandee jumped in again with her own bid, bringing a cheer from the crowd.

Gina reflexively upped her.

"Better be careful," Ross said. "You don't want to win."

Mandee shot her a look of pure annoyance and bid higher.

Everyone's attention went to the readout board.

No new bids came up.

"Sold!" Mandee called out gleefully, bringing her hammer down.

"She should have waited," Ross said with a frown. "A couple of them would have jumped back in."

"She wanted it for herself." Gina was sure of that.

A waiter offered her more champagne, and she took it.

"Well, you dodged a bullet then," her brother said. "You might have been the one shelling out the money."

Gina took a swallow. "True." She tried to look relieved at the turn of events.

By the end of all thirty-two cowboys, the Chamber of Commerce had made an enormous sum of money.

Lila was the first to congratulate Gina, giving her an ecstatic hug and telling her she should do more project management, since she so obviously had a talent for it. Many in the audience stuck around to mix and mingle, and virtually all the business owners who stood to benefit from the fundraising congratulated Gina on the accomplishment.

There was one notable exception. Rafe didn't appear. By the time Gina broke free and went to look for him, he was gone, leaving her to wonder what their sexy interlude had meant to him.

* * *

Gina had bid on him.

Two mornings later, Rafe told himself not to read anything into it. He wouldn't be so conceited as to think their kiss had something to do with it.

She was just helping to amp up the crowd. After all, she'd let Mandee win in the end. She could have upped the celebrity reporter's bid if she'd been that interested in spending the day with him.

Rafe would have loved to spend the day with Gina, but instead he got Mandee. He was trying not to dread it.

Maybe he wasn't being fair. He didn't know Mandee, not really. Sure, he'd watched her a few times on *Royal Tonight!* and he didn't care for the way she badgered guests and tried to score cheap laughs by embarrassing them. But that was her television persona. She could be a perfectly nice woman.

JJ appeared in the empty RCW kitchen, seeming surprised to spot Rafe coming down the short staircase from his office.

"You're here early, boss."

Rafe entered the kitchen, meeting JJ over the long prep counter.

"I wanted to sign off on payroll," he said. "I've got a full day today."

"What's up?"

"Heading out to the ranch."

"Ahhh…" the chef said with a gleam in his eyes. "The date with the pretty TV woman. That explains your outfit."

"It's not a *date*. It's a day on the ranch. You think she's pretty?"

"Sure, she's pretty. Though I guess they can make anyone look pretty on television. I wonder what she looks like without all that makeup. Maybe you'll find out."

"I doubt it." He poured himself a cup of coffee then held the pot up to JJ as a question.

"Sure...thanks." JJ grinned. "You guys really raked it in on that auction."

"We did. More than I expected, that's for sure."

"Is it enough?"

"Enough for what?"

"Well, to pull RCW out of the fire for one."

Rafe paused. He'd been thinking about that, growing less and less comfortable with the idea of taking charity to save his restaurant.

"Boss?" JJ prompted, seeming confused by Rafe's silence.

"When I started this place—" he looked around the spotless kitchen "—I swore I would make or break it on my own merits."

"And you did."

"So far. But this...getting free money from a charity event. It doesn't sit right."

"You lost money because of a crime. That's not on merit. You deserve to get some of it back. That's just justice."

"I've been thinking..." Rafe didn't want to risk RCW's future. The very last thing he wanted to do was lose the restaurant and force his employees to find new jobs. But maybe there was some middle ground.

"You're making me nervous," JJ said.

"What are our options? I mean our *other* options. If we had to pull ourselves up by our bootstraps, get creative and use nothing but RCW resources, how might we do it?"

"Hmm." JJ leaned back against a wall and seemed to contemplate. "First place I'd look is unused capacity."

"We don't open until eleven," Rafe noted. "Breakfast?"

"That's one idea, the most obvious idea."

"What do you think of it?" he asked.

"We'd need a whole new shift of employees. Plus a new menu, marketing…competition's really stiff at the breakfast hour."

"People might not like such a formal place for breakfast." Rafe knew RCW was a destination, an experience. It wasn't necessarily someplace for a quick short stack and fried eggs.

"What if we focused on the kitchen only?" JJ asked.

"How so?"

"This might sound self-serving…but what about my mom and sisters?"

Rafe was confused.

"Mom's an amazing cook."

"Most moms are." He thought of his own mother and his nana's delicious homemade specialties.

"She bakes. She plays with her old family recipes to create fusion desserts, and they're in demand at the recreation center, at church, for my sisters' sports teams."

Rafe could guess where this was going. "Are you suggesting she's ready to go commercial?"

"I think she is. I'd have to ask her. But she could use the kitchen from, say, four a.m. to midmorning, try to get some contracts with local grocery retailers and do a split of the profits."

As Rafe thought his way through the idea, he caught

sight of the wall clock and realized he was behind schedule.

"You don't like it," JJ said, obviously catching Rafe's frown. "Forget I suggested it."

"No," he corrected him. "I think it has merit. But I'm running late. I gotta go." He started for the door to the dining room where he could cut through to the parking lot, but then abruptly looked back over his shoulder. "Would your mom bake me some samples?"

"She'd love to. Business opportunity or not, she'd be thrilled to bake for you."

Rafe grinned and gave the chef a parting thumbs-up as he rushed to the parking lot.

He hopped in his SUV and headed for the highway. Given the amount of money Mandee had paid for her ranch day, Rafe was determined not to be late.

He swung into the ranch yard with five minutes to spare.

Mandee was already there, chatting with Matias on the shaded front porch. Her outfit was almost glaringly bright, but Rafe supposed it must look good on camera. In his worn blue jeans, steel-gray shirt and a battered brown Stetson, he was perfectly happy to fade into the background.

He strode up to them, pasting a smile on his face. "Good morning, Mandee. Welcome to the Cortez-Williams Ranch."

She grinned back, while Matias smirked at Rafe from behind her back.

Rafe gave his brother a look that told him he was going down next.

Matias's experience had been sold to an online bidder named Anastasia Kovell from Boston who was due to arrive in Royal in a few days. Rafe and his brothers had taken bets on her age. With a name like Anastasia, Rafe had put his money on her being sixty-seven. Matias was going to have to be careful she didn't break a bone or something.

"Mom's put out coffee and honey cornbread muffins," Matias said.

Rafe looked to Mandee. "Hungry?"

"That sounds great," she answered enthusiastically. "Will your family mind if I take pictures inside?"

Rafe shrugged. "Shouldn't be a problem." He couldn't see anyone caring if their dining room made the internet.

Seven

When Gina saw the first photo of Rafe and Mandee pop up on her phone at ten o'clock in the morning, she knew it was going to be a long day. The pair looked annoyingly happy, sipping coffee and eating muffins with melting butter.

"Try the lemon curd," Sarabeth said, waving her hand toward one of the half dozen little cakes on the table in front of them at Best Baked. The specialty bakery was conveniently located next door to Natalie Valentine's Bridal Shop, where they were headed next.

Gina told herself to set thoughts of Rafe and Mandee aside. She should be grateful for the distraction of wedding shopping with her mother today. "Are you sure eating cake before trying on dresses is a good idea?"

"It's the *best* idea," Sarabeth said, taking another bite of the vanilla lemon curd cake. "Yum. This one is definitely in the running." She pushed the mini cake and a knife in her daughter's direction. "That way, we can pick dresses that leave us room to eat at the reception."

Gina couldn't help but appreciate her mother's logic.

She cut herself a thin slice of the cake and transferred it to a small plate, taking up a dainty silver fork to have a taste. The cake was moist and sweet, while the lemon curd layer was creamy smooth with just enough tang for balance.

"Oh, yes," she sighed with approval, taking a second bite to confirm. "Do we even have to try the others?"

"Of course we have to try the others. All of them. How often does a woman get a free-for-all with cake?"

Gina's phone chimed. She'd set up an alert for posts from Rafe and Mandee's experience. Gina told herself it was part of her job as project manager. She needed to ensure each of the cowboy experiences was a success.

Mandee's outing with Rafe was the first one on the calendar, since the reporter was local and also very eager. As far as Gina knew, nobody else was planning to live-share their day. But if they did, she'd told herself she'd keep tabs on them, too.

She picked up her phone to see what was happening on the ranch. Breakfast seemed to be over. They'd moved on to the horse barn and were tacking up. Mandee looked glorious in a pair of burgundy jeans and a patterned shirt of burgundy, silver and white that was fitted perfectly to her slim curves. Topping off the outfit was a pair of Western boots and a gleaming white Stetson. The crowning touch was a big silver belt buckle at her waist.

Gina wondered if *Royal Tonight!* had specifically coordinated the dramatic outfit.

"Not the carrot. No." Sarabeth's words brought Gina back to the present. She was wrinkling her lips and scowling.

Gina set down her phone. "I guess I can skip that one then."

"Have a bite to confirm my opinion."

"Sure." Gina reached for the carrot cake, determined to please the bride.

In Gina's opinion, everything about wedding planning ought to be fun. It wasn't just a day or a weekend, it was a whole experience leading up to the ceremony and the reception—the cake, the dress, the flowers. She looked forward to doing it herself one day, maybe... hopefully.

Until then, she was her mother's go-to gal for this wedding, and she was determined to do a fantastic job.

In the end, they settled on the vanilla lemon curd and chose a white chocolate frosting with a spray of butter yellow flowers cascading down the multitiered cake. It had to be large given the number of guests invited to the wedding. But it would be elegant without looking too fussy.

As they walked down the block to Natalie Valentine's, Gina surreptitiously checked her phone.

If the video clip Mandee had uploaded was any indication, the horseback ride was a hit. They were walking their horses along the banks of the river, lush green trees flanking the trail and giving them some shade. Rafe looked sexy and at home in the saddle. Mandee's form left something to be desired, but it obviously wasn't her first time on a horse.

Rafe was laughing, looking like he was having a great time. Maybe they were having a great conversation. Maybe he thought Mandee was beautiful dressed up like that. Maybe he was glad she had won the auction.

Gina hated the jealousy that surged within her. But *she* wanted to be the one Rafe rode horses with, talked with, laughed with. She should have bid higher.

"Have you thought about a color for your dress?" Sarabeth asked as she pulled open the door to the wedding shop.

Gina guiltily tucked her phone away. "I'm flexible. What did you decide for the flowers?"

"With an ivory dress, I thought cream and pale yellow, maybe a bit of green to set things off."

"I like it."

"Hello, Sarabeth." A smiling thirtyish woman— Mary, according to her name tag—came their way. "Your timing is perfect."

The shop was light and airy with a long row of wedding gowns on one wall and a rainbow of bridesmaid and flower-girl dresses. The back of the shop featured large opulent changing rooms and curved full-length mirrors.

"I've got a sketch all ready for you," Mary said, indicating a round table with four plush chairs. "Please, get comfortable."

"This is going to be fun," Sarabeth said, moving eagerly to the table.

"You can see the sweetheart neckline," Mary pointed with the tip of her pencil. "Cap sleeves, like we talked about. We can play with the length."

"I love it," Sarabeth said with a wide grin. "You got it just right."

In her handbag, Gina's phone chimed another subtle alert.

A younger woman appeared from the back of the shop, approaching them with glasses of white wine on a silver tray. "Can I offer you a chardonnay?"

"Yes, please," Sarabeth said.

"I'm in," Gina said.

Not a date, she reminded herself, even if it did look like they were totally into each other. It was a cowboy experience. She could only hope Mandee didn't experience too much of Rafe before it was all over.

Mary opened a book pointed to a swatch of lace. "I was thinking of this one." She pointed. "Or—" she turned two pages over "—this?"

Sarabeth leaned forward to study the two options, and Gina slipped her phone out of her purse for a peek.

On the little phone screen, Rafe and Mandee had dismounted and the horses were drinking from the river. Mandee was showing off a bouquet of wildflowers to the camera, bringing them to her face for a sniff. Since she was the focus of the video, it was hard to see Rafe's expression.

Next there was a photo of Rafe with a quirky smile. The old windmill was in the background, catapulting Gina back to her kiss with him there, the moment his lips had touched hers, and her world seemed to fill up with sunlight.

"Oh, that I like," Sarabeth enthused. "What do you think, Gina?"

Gina looked back up, quickly orienting herself to the swatch book and seeing a delicate ivory lace pattern of leaves and vines. "Nice," she quickly agreed.

Annoyed with her wandering attention, she stuffed her phone back into her purse.

"Time for you to get to work," Sarabeth said to her,

pointing with her wineglass to the array of bridesmaid dresses.

"I have some ideas." Mary came to her feet. "After I did your sketch, a few of our new styles jumped out at me." She marched over to the wall of dresses, swiftly choosing a peach, a mint green and a butter yellow dress.

Sarabeth got comfortable in her cushy chair. "Give me a fashion show."

Gina took a bracing drink of the chardonnay and came to her feet.

It took over an hour of changing, laughing, twirling and sipping wine to find the right dress. But when Gina walked out for the final time, she knew it was the one, and Sarabeth obviously knew that as well.

It was a strapless chiffon of pale seafoam, skewing blue in some lighting, green in others, with a sweetheart neckline and a snug wraparound bodice that flattered her waistline. The skirt fell softly to land four inches above her knee. She had no less than a dozen pairs of shoes that would work with it.

"Well, *there* you go," Sarabeth said with a smile.

"That'll work," Mary said with a nod. "And we can do other colors."

"I like it just like this." Her mom stood, walked closer and tilted her head. "It brings out the green in her eyes."

"I've got some jade-and-gold earrings," Gina said. "Or just some little diamond studs." She drew back her hair. "Half up, half down, you were saying?"

"You'll need just the right necklace," Sarabeth told her. "Show me what you're wearing, and I'll find something that coordinates."

"Or we could go shopping." Her mom's eyes lit up. "I haven't bought you a bridesmaid gift yet."

"You don't need to—"

"Oh yes, I do," Sarabeth said firmly.

"Something delicate," Mary said. "Yellow gold would be better than platinum."

"You can't go wrong with diamonds," Sarabeth said.

"Mom, you *can't*."

"I want you to have a keepsake, honey. I want you to remember this your whole life."

"I'm never going to forget your wedding." The unbridled love Gina had felt for her mother when she was a little girl came suddenly spilling back. All their trials and tribulations, and the separation that had kept them apart for so many years, fell away.

Her throat clogged. "I love you, Mom."

Sarabeth pulled her into a warm hug. "I love you, too, honey." Then she stood back, her eyes shining. "You'll knock 'em dead in that dress."

Gina gave a brave smile, wondering who exactly she'd knock dead since she didn't even have a date. Her traitorous mind turned to Rafe again, picturing him out on the range in his blue jeans, then at the restaurant in his finely fitted suit. He was definitely a guy you could take anywhere.

The Edmond Organization was covering the hard costs for each of the cowboy experiences.

Gina could have paid the RCW dinner tab tomorrow or the next day or even next week. But when a picture of a candlelit dinner for Rafe and Mandee at a cozy RCW table came up on her phone, Gina decided punctuality was more important.

She left home, driving across town to park in the RCW lot. She had no way of knowing if both Rafe and Mandee were still inside laughing over dinner and their day. The photo had shown them finishing up a chocolate soufflé, but maybe they were lingering over brandy now.

On the other hand, maybe they'd already left RCW. If they had, she'd never know if they went together or separately. And wouldn't that just mess with her mind.

But she'd come this far. She braced herself and headed for the front entrance, passing through the double doorway into the dark, richly appointed lobby.

"Good evening," the hostess greeted her with a smile from behind a narrow desk.

Moving forward, Gina craned her neck to scan the main dining room. No Rafe there, only a few diners in the flickering firelight among some empty tables.

"Are you meeting someone tonight?" the hostess asked pleasantly, coming out from behind the little counter. "I'm afraid we can't seat a new party after ten."

"I was looking for Rafe."

"Mr. Cortez-Williams?"

"Yes," she answered.

"I'm not sure he's still here. Can you wait here a minute? I'll check."

"Thanks."

Gina waited a few minutes, considered leaving, then stuck around a few minutes more. She told herself she was here to pay the tab, nothing more, nothing less. If Rafe had already gone, she'd thank the hostess for her help. But if Rafe was still here, and Mandee was with him… Well, she would still hand over her credit card and slink home in disappointment, knowing the cowboy experience had turned into a real date.

"Gina?" Rafe appeared in the archway from the dining room, looking surprised to see her. His shirtsleeves were rolled up and his tie was loose. Whatever he was doing, it was a lot more casual than dinner.

"Sorry to disturb you," she said, trying to surreptitiously check behind him for signs of Mandee. "Are you busy?"

"No. What are you doing here?"

She swallowed, trying for an offhand look. "Edmond is paying the tab, remember?"

He looked confused. "You're here for the check?"

She nodded. "Yes. I'm…uh…trying to…you know."

"Be ridiculously punctual?"

She nodded. "I don't like to leave things hanging."

"Sure," he said, still looking confused, but also looking deliciously disheveled and oh so sexy.

They both went quiet. After a moment, she could feel the hostess's curious gaze.

"I can give you my credit card," Gina offered, going for her purse.

He canted his head into the dining room. "Come on in."

She hesitated, sorely tempted to follow him, but wanting to keep up the facade that she was only here to pay the bill.

He started to walk away, and she had only seconds to make her decision.

With a quick thank-you to the hostess, she followed. He led the way through the swinging kitchen door into a wave of fragrant warmth where the cooking staff was clearing and cleaning.

The two of them skirted the edge of the kitchen before climbing a short staircase.

Rafe pushed open a door and stood back to let her pass.

She walked into what was obviously his office. It was surprisingly large and airy, especially for a room accessed via the kitchen. But then she saw a second door and realized they'd taken a back route.

His desk was at one end of the rectangular room. It was honey oak with clean lines and a low-back chair. In front of the desk were two light brown leather armchairs that looked very comfortable. There was also a six-person meeting table in the inside corner and a small conversation group with four armchairs and a low square table next to windows that looked out on the lush greenbelt.

The door clicked shut behind Rafe.

"This is really nice," Gina said, glancing around.

"You bid on me," Rafe murmured without preamble, a thread of amusement in his tone.

He caught her off guard, and she turned back. "I was only making a point."

His brow went up in a challenge. "That point being?"

"Mandee wasn't supposed to bid. None of us were. We wanted as much money as possible to come from outside the community."

"Her money is as good as anyone's," he said easily.

Gina didn't have a counter to that. "How did today go?"

Rafe shrugged his wide shoulders. "It went. I don't believe you."

"Don't believe me about what?"

He eased closer, a glint of determination in his eyes. "Why you said you bid on me."

She felt herself rise to the challenge. "Oh, yeah? Why do *you* think I bid on your cowboy experience?"

"Because you wanted it."

"Aren't you full of yourself."

"I didn't say you wanted me." But his heated gaze moved to her lips.

She wasn't about to admit anything. "You're saying I wanted a horseback ride?"

"Yes."

"I have a stable of my own."

"I guess you also wanted to meet the foals and calves and walk through the Cortez-Williams Ranch."

"Don't forget the cattle herding."

"Or the dinner," he said, leaning in, his voice dropping lower. "Admit it, Gina. You wanted to experience *this* cowboy."

His deep tone and sensual words vibrated through her, bringing desire, want and passion to life.

"Good news," he said, brushing his hand against hers.

She shivered in reaction, barely getting the words out. "What news?"

"There's a second prize."

She desperately hoped second prize was another kiss in Rafe's arms. "What is it?" she managed, easing closer, waiting for a witty comeback.

"The muffins, the foals, the cattle drive, the whole experience."

She drew back far enough to focus on him. "Huh?"

"You pay the amount of your last bid, and I'll do it all over again."

She realized they were having two different conversations. Could she have misread him that badly? "You want my money?"

"I do."

"And you'll take me cattle-herding?"

"I will."

She squelched her disappointment, telling herself to get real, get grounded, and deal with the fact that her intense infatuation wasn't reciprocated.

He liked her, she assured herself. He at least *liked* her. So, maybe their kisses didn't blow his mind the way they blew hers, and maybe he wasn't as desperate to fall into each other's arms all over again, but he must at least like her a little bit.

"What if I want something else?" she asked, thinking that if she was going to bargain for his time, she might as well get what she really needed.

"What? You mean like a picnic or a swim in the river?"

"I need a date."

"Well…we'd do the dinner thing at the end."

She shook her head. "To my mother's wedding. I need a date to my mother's wedding."

He tilted his head, his eyes narrowing. "You want to pay me to escort you to your mother's wedding?"

"No! I want to pay the Chamber of Commerce fundraiser for a cowboy experience. I just happen to want a *different* cowboy experience."

A slow smile grew on his face. "Are you under the impression we can customize, ma'am?"

"You can if you want my money, sir."

He gave a chopped chuckle. "Sure."

"You'll do it?"

"For you, Gina, I'll do just about anything." The sensual gleam was back in his eyes, but she didn't trust it this time.

"In the meantime," he continued, his eyes darkening further as he brushed his fingertips over her cheek, bending his head, moving in. "Is there any *other* kind of cowboy experience that might interest you?"

"I—"

"Just say yes, Princess."

"Yes."

In an instant, he was kissing her, his hot, tender lips slanting over hers, opening, deepening.

She moaned in relief, her arms encircling his neck to anchor her while her blood sang with happiness and her bones all but melted.

Rafe wrapped his arms around her waist, firmly tugging her against his body, holding her strong and steady. He kissed her lips, then her neck, then her shoulder, pushing the cap sleeve of her dress out of the way so he could have better access.

She splayed her hands on his warm chest, sliding her palms from his pecs to his washboard stomach, frustrated by the thin barrier of his shirt. Needing *more*, she started on the buttons, and he muttered something under his breath. Then she heard the lock click on the door behind him.

He grasped the tails of his shirt and pulled, popping the buttons, sending them scattering as he tore the cotton garment from his shoulders.

She gazed at his magnificent body for a few moments, but then they were back in each other's arms with their kisses growing frenzied.

Rafe pressed his hands to her back, her rear, moving

down her thighs, massaging his way to the hem of her dress. Then she gasped as his fingertips touched her bare skin. She came up on her toes, running her palms over his shoulders, reveling in the strength and definition she found there. Emboldened, she kissed her way across his pecs, leaving damp circles as she moved to his neck.

His hands came to her lacy silk panties and she shuddered with desire, her teeth biting gently down on him. He stripped off her panties, dropping them to the floor. Then he lifted her to his waist, her thighs wrapping around him, her body brushing erotically against his pants.

He moved then, carrying her, kissing her deeply as they crossed the few paces to his desk.

Perched on the edge, she stripped off her dress, meeting his eyes for a long, hot moment as she sat naked in front of him. He brushed back her hair, framed her face with his hands, kissed her tenderly, long and deep, then his hand moved to cup her breast.

Gina moaned again, arching backward, letting sharp sensations of pleasure race to her core. She wanted him, *badly*, and she reached for his pants, popping the button and sliding down the zipper.

"Gina," he groaned in her ear, dragging her close, producing a condom. "Yes. Oh, yes."

"Rafe," she moaned in return, gasping as he entered her.

His breathing went deeper as he thrust, becoming ragged as he sped up.

Hers did, too, lungs laboring as if there wasn't enough oxygen in the room.

She clung to him, passion coursing through her belly,

her thighs, to the tips of her toes and roots of her hair. Her nipples hardened, grazing his chest, as his motion increased again. A roar came up in her ears and light glowed around the edges of her eyes.

Digging his fingertips into her hair, he kissed her deeper and harder. Then he scooped one hand beneath her, holding her fast against his rhythm.

She could feel the world falling away, night turning into day and back to night again as she floated free, stars sparkling all around. His breath brushed her ear, and he called out her name, lifting her up against him as the stars swirled against black sky, coalescing then bursting into wave after wave of bright energy.

Her pulse pounded in her ears.

Rafe held her close, cradling her head and her back as he gently set her back down on the desk.

Her heart rate settled, syncing with his.

"Wow," he muttered.

"Wow," she answered.

He drew back just far enough to focus on her face. "I didn't plan…"

She shook her head. "Me, either."

He paused. "Too soon for a cowboy experience joke?"

She cracked a smile.

He gathered her into a hug again. "I really didn't mean for this to happen. I mean, sure, I wanted to kiss you. I'm human, and you're spectacular. But I don't want you to think I lured you up here to take advantage."

He hadn't taken advantage of *anything*, but she didn't know for sure what he was saying. She found herself parsing his words again, worrying that the lovemaking had meant something different for her than for him.

"It's fine," she said, attempting an air of nonchalance.

He eased back and she reached for her dress, swiftly pulling it over her head to cover up. While she slipped off the desk, Rafe adjusted his pants.

Her purse was around here somewhere, and she tracked it down. Finding a comb, she fixed her hair before refreshing her lipstick, all of which made her feel somewhat more together.

Clearly, they weren't going to hang around and whisper secrets in the afterglow, so she dug out her credit card as reality crowded in. There were still staff and maybe even some customers outside in the restaurant and kitchen. She suddenly wanted to get that walk over with, get back in her car and get safely home.

She turned to find Rafe still shirtless, a sheen of sweat on his chest as he braced himself back against his desk. She focused on his forehead, wanting to avoid his sexy body and preferring not to look him straight in the eyes.

She held out her card. "Can you run this through?"

He looked confused.

"For the dinner," she clarified.

His confusion turned to indignation. "You still want to pay for the dinner?"

"That was the deal. Edmond will pay hard costs. You put in the sweat equity."

"It's my restaurant," he said.

"And you've lost a lot of money because of this whole thing." She pushed the credit card closer.

"I'm not taking it."

She didn't know why he was acting like this. "Don't be so proud."

"Don't *you* be so patronizing."

"Rafe." The last thing she wanted was for him to treat her differently because they'd just had sex. And not just *any* sex. Wild and crazy, impulsive sex. She'd burned for him, and he'd given her what she craved, but now he just looked…angry.

"No," he said with finality.

"Fine," she said, putting the card away.

She turned.

"Wait." The anger in his voice was gone.

But she reached for the door anyway, needing this episode to be over.

"Gina." His footsteps sounded behind her.

She quickly pulled the door open and slipped out, counting on the fact that he'd have to put his shirt on before he could try to chase her down.

Eight

Rafe knew he'd messed up with Gina. But the last thing he needed in that moment—still reeling from their earth-shattering lovemaking—was a reminder of the stark differences between them. He couldn't bring himself to take her charity last night. And he still felt the same way today.

The businesses that invested in Soiree on the Bay were well represented in the Chamber of Commerce conference room this morning. Lila was at the lectern organizing her notes as the stragglers wandered in and took their seats. Rafe had caught a fleeting glimpse of Gina far across the room, causing his chest to hitch in regret. She hadn't seen him yet, and he knew it was better that way.

Someone pulled out a chair at his table, and he looked up to see Lorenzo.

"Hey," his brother said as he sat down, a cup of coffee in his hand.

Rafe pulled his thoughts from Gina. "How're you doing?"

"Did you hear?" Lorenzo sounded serious.

"What?" Rafe braced himself for family news, maybe an accident on the ranch.

"On top of everything else, Billy Holmes is trolling Rusty."

Rafe's initial relief that nobody had been hurt was quickly replaced by confusion. Why would a man on the run from the law post anything on social media? "Are they sure it's him?"

"They seem to think it's him. Valencia was talking to Lila, who was talking to Lani Li. Lani's still following the case closely."

"What's he posting?" Rafe was beginning to think Billy wasn't the brightest guy in the world. Then again, maybe he was blinded by emotion right now, because he'd certainly been smart when he'd hidden the embezzled money.

"Taunts about Rusty, how all this could have been avoided if Rusty had only treated him fairly. He's got a bone to pick with the Edmonds, that's for sure."

"So all this was about getting back at his father?"

"Looks like."

"Disappointment in your family is no excuse for a crime spree."

Lorenzo gave a snort of derision. "If it was, that's all anybody'd have time for."

Rafe quirked a smile and shook his head at his brother's dark humor. "Billy's oh-poor-me victim crap is ridiculous. The guy should confront Rusty if that's what it takes, but give the innocent bystanders back their money."

"Valencia's horse rescue could sure use it. Billy knew all the good the proceeds were going to do. What kind of a man takes money away from troubled kids to…what…buy gold fixtures for his condo in the Maldives?"

Rafe shook his head at that, too. "I hope we never find him." He paused. "I mean, I hope the Cortez-Williams brothers never find themselves alone in a back alley with the guy. The money, I want back."

It was Lorenzo's turn to smile.

"Can I have your attention?" Lila asked from the front of the room. Her voice was strong but not overpowering through the microphone.

People settled. Everyone was interested in what she had to say about the results of the auction.

Rafe glanced at Gina again. He could see her profile, her glossy hair, neat now, not like it was after he'd run his fingers through it making love to her. She was wearing a shimmering peach blouse and a dark blazer over a pair of tan slacks. She looked professional, but somehow more comfortably so than in the past. He supposed her success had done that for her. She had to be feeling hugely confident in her capabilities right now.

"—owe a big thank-you to Gina Edmond."

The mention of her name rocked Rafe back to reality.

The room burst into enthusiastic applause, and Rafe quickly joined in.

Gina rose to her feet to give the crowd a wave of thanks. As her gaze swung around the room, it caught on Rafe's. She paused for a second and her smile faltered. But then she recovered, finished the turn and sat down.

His regret deepened.

"The auction was an amazing fundraiser, and while we're a long way from recouping all the losses, I'm happy to announce we can refund about fifteen percent of the initial investment to each of the impacted businesses."

There was a murmur of disappointment that turned into lukewarm applause. Rafe's heart went out to Gina. She'd worked so hard to make as much as she had. Nobody could have done better, no way.

"Well, that's that," Lorenzo muttered, sounding distinctly exasperated.

Rafe looked to his brother, intent on defending Gina. "Fifteen percent isn't nothing."

"Fifteen percent of the investment doesn't help Valencia."

Rafe understood his brother's disappointment. He was also reminded that organizations beyond the investors had lost out, too. Many people in Royal had been hit hard by Billy's crimes, harder even than Rafe himself had been hit.

He made a split-second decision and came to his feet.

Lila looked curiously his way.

"I'm donating my fifteen percent," he called out, hoping to inspire others. "RCW will recover on its own. People will keep dining, keep celebrating special occasions and continue to take special evenings out. It'll take some time, but we'll manage. Other organizations might not be so lucky. Others were counting on this event to do good and important work, more important than feeding sambal shrimp and cranberry apple pastry to people with disposable cash."

He saw the crowd was listening with curiosity, some of them more suspicious than curious, including both Ross and Asher Edmond. Rafe realized he should get to his point. "I'm donating RCW's fifteen percent to Donovan Horse Rescue."

He caught Lorenzo's shocked expression from the corner of his eye.

"That's very generous of you, Rafe," Lila said.

He sat down.

"What the heck, bro?" Lorenzo asked.

"She can use the money."

"But RCW…it's in trouble."

Rafe gave a shrug. "We've been brainstorming and have some ideas. We'll dig ourselves out of this hole."

"Take the money," Lorenzo said.

"You take the money. Valencia deserves it. I made a bad investment, and I'm paying the price. But I'm strong and smart and hardworking, and I don't need the Edmonds or anyone else to take pity on me." Rafe's voice had grown fiercer at the end of the statement.

Lorenzo drew back, looking more confused than ever. "You feel that strongly about it?"

"I do."

"Well, Valencia is sure going to be your best friend."

"Good." Rafe said. "I like Valencia." His brother's fiancée was one of the best people he'd ever met. They were lucky to have her joining the family.

Conversation had resumed in the room. Lila had left the lectern and was circulating, answering questions.

Rafe dared to glance Gina's way again and found

her surrounded by business owners. It was clear they
were congratulating her, and he was happy about that.
She deserved their thanks.

Gina didn't know what Rafe had been thinking at
this morning's Chamber of Commerce meeting, but he'd
made a big mistake. She'd gone back to the Edmond of-
fices after the meeting, but all day long she'd worried
that his anger with her might have pushed him to make a
bad decision—a decision detrimental to RCW's future.

Feeling responsible, she'd looked for him at the
steakhouse, even though she dreaded the idea of going
back into his office. But she needed to talk to him, to
change his mind about taking the money.

He hadn't been there, so now she was trying his
home.

Gina had never been to Rafe's house before, but she
was familiar with the neighborhood. She knew it was
exclusive, and that some houses had amazing views of
Pine Valley. She pulled around the crescent, located
his address and turned into the driveway. There was a
garage directly in front of her and she could see that a
set of rounded concrete steps led to an oversize wooden
door with etched-glass windows on either side, cut in diamond panes with gold filler. The front yard was nicely
sized and well-trimmed, landscaped in shrubs rather
than flower beds.

Gina stepped out of her car and made her way
through the hot, humid air toward the door, gathering her courage along the way. She rang the bell and
stepped back to wait. Glancing behind her, she took
note of the other nice houses along the street. They were
well spaced and very well cared for. The crescent was

bordered with sidewalks, the driveways finished with exposed aggregate. It was an overly civilized neighborhood—a far cry from the blowing fields, paddocks and hills of the Cortez-Williams Ranch.

The door opened, and Gina turned back, taking in the sight of Rafe in the middle of the doorway wearing faded jeans with an olive-green T-shirt stretched across his chest. She'd expected a suit. She didn't know why.

"Gina?" He was clearly confused by her appearance.

She shook herself back to her purpose. "Why did you do it?"

"Do what?"

"You know what! The money. You need the money."

He drew himself up. "*Will* you stop worrying about my finances?"

"I can't stop worrying about your finances. I'm the problem with your finances."

He crossed his arms over his chest. "You have nothing to do with my finances."

"See?" She pointed at him. "See that right there? *That's* the problem."

He cocked his head and stared at her for a moment. "Did that make sense inside your head?"

"Don't play dumb."

"I'm not playing anything."

"Rafe, you flipped out the other night when I tried to pay—"

"Is this going to be a long conversation?" he asked.

"I don't know. I didn't think it all the way through."

He stepped back and gestured her inside.

She decided that was a good idea, since the alternative was standing out here on the front porch. She was a long, long way from being a celebrity, but there were people in Royal who would recognize her, and she'd rather not get questions about why she'd been arguing with Rafe on his front porch.

She walked inside, and he closed the door behind her.

"Carry on," he said, making a sweeping gesture with one arm.

It took her a split second to remember what she'd been saying. "When I tried to pay for dinner the other night, you flipped out."

"Because I own the restaurant, and it was unnecessary."

She peered into his eyes. "You're lying. For some reason, you don't want my money. Then today…" It was her turn to make a sweeping arm gesture. "Today, you turned down tens of thousands of dollars! You can't afford to do that."

"You have absolutely no idea what I can and can't afford."

"Why, Rafe? Am I so tainted?"

"Don't be dramatic. Everything's not all about you, Princess."

"You're picking a fight." She couldn't help but interpret that as a defense mechanism.

"I don't need to *pick* a fight. You're having one all by yourself," he pointed out.

"Take the money, Rafe."

"I don't need the money, Gina."

"I know you took out a second mortgage," she told him. "Everyone knows that."

"Well, that's none of everyone's business."

"Are you that proud?" The jut of his chin told her he was. "It's not *my* money, Rafe. It's raised money, and you helped raise it."

"You and your brothers kicked in."

"Because the Edmonds brought Billy to town. That makes it partly our responsibility."

"Maybe." He shrugged. "But I chose to invest in Soiree on the Bay. I took a risk, and that part is my responsibility."

She dropped her purse on a side table. "Forget pride, that's just plain stubbornness." Then she found herself looking around.

He had a wonderful house, spacious and tastefully decorated but not ostentatious. It was lighter than she'd expected, with open beam ceilings in the living room and high peaked windows showing a view of the valley. She saw four modern taupe leather chairs around a glass coffee table. Knowing Rafe's background, she would have expected dark armchairs and heavy wood side tables. In the corners, he had large, leafy, freestanding plants.

She took an unconscious step forward, curious to see more. "This is really nice."

"I'm *not* stubborn," he said.

"You're impossible," she retorted, but she walked past him into the living room and took in the pot lighting and a pale mosaic glass-fronted fireplace. "You live here?"

"Is that a serious question?"

She took a few more steps and found a formal dining room that seated eight. "It doesn't look like you."

He had followed her along. "Maybe you don't know me very well."

She had to admit, she really didn't.

"Ask me," he said.

"Ask you what?"

"Ask me why I don't need the money."

There was an archway leading from the side of the dining room, and she couldn't resist walking through it to the kitchen. His counters were gray marble, the cupboards white, and a small dining nook had a table set with—

She paused. "Are you having a party?"

The kitchen table was covered in the most delicious-looking baked goods. Her nose perked up at the tantalizing smells—banana, brown sugar, coconut and peanut butter.

"I'm not having a party. Ask me why I don't need the money." He'd come up close behind her, closer than was comfortable but still too far away.

She wanted to lean back against him, wanted his arms to come around her, wanted to turn in his arms and kiss his sexy mouth and—

"Want to help?" he asked.

The question threw her. She craned her neck to look back at him.

He nodded to the table. "JJ's mom made those."

"Did you decide on a bake sale?"

"No, we're not having a bake sale. Those are for me."

"To *eat*? No offense, Rafe, I mean you're trim now, but that won't last long if you dig into all this."

He chuckled. "I'm not going to eat *all* of them. They're for taste-testing. You could give me your opinion."

The invitation was beyond tempting.

"Come on," he said, gesturing to the bright little nook.

Who could say no to an offer like that?

They sat down opposite each other at the kitchen

table, bathed in the long rays of the western sunlight. Rafe handed her a fork, a spoon and a little knife along with a dessert plate.

"Sarabeth and I did this earlier in the week with wedding cake," she said as he set a slice of banana raspberry cake on her plate and then his.

"So you're experienced."

"I'm half a pound heavier."

He grinned. "Did you find one?"

"We did. Vanilla cake with lemon curd filling and white chocolate frosting. And the design is gorgeous— classic white, pale yellow flowers with a little mint green."

He took a bite of the banana cake. "And how does this stack up?"

"Not quite as elaborate," Gina said before taking a taste. The flavors all but exploded in her mouth. The sweet banana was balanced by the tangy raspberries, and there was a light honey glaze that lingered delightfully on her tongue. "*Oh*, it's unique."

"Isn't it?"

She tried another bite.

"Pace yourself," Rafe warned with a little wave of his fork.

She grinned self-consciously. "I can't resist."

He took another bite himself, despite his advice to her. "How about something savory instead of sweet?"

She gazed around the table at the various dishes, spotting something that looked like an herb puff. "What about that one?"

He held out the bowl. "Help yourself."

She did, and so did he.

The puffs were light and airy with threads of tangy

cheese, garden herbs, dried peppers and tomatoes. They moved on to a cheese tart, a rolled pastry layered with pistachio and lemon chutney. Everything was fresh, unique and wonderful.

As Gina used her fingertips to take a final nibble of the pastry layer, Rafe sat back, his voice going low and sultry. "Ask me."

The atmosphere suddenly shifted, and her attention moved from the baking to Rafe. Her chest tightened and her pulse sped up as her brain considered the possibilities. "Ask you what?"

"Why I don't need the money."

She ordered her fantasies back from the brink. They were still talking about money, nothing more, nothing else. She sucked the tiny crumbs from her fingers. "Why don't you need the money?"

He nodded to the table. "We're going to sell these."

"You're extending the menu?" She was puzzled. She'd liked everything, *loved* everything, really, even if some of the exotic flavors seemed slightly out of step with the traditional steakhouse. But she didn't see it changing the company's cash flow in any meaningful way.

He shook his head. "JJ's mom. She's going to use the kitchen in the off hours and start a whole new line of business."

Gina sat back in her chair. "That's…"

"Smart?"

"Innovative, really innovative. Smart, too."

"It was JJ's idea. He came at it from the perspective of unused capacity."

"You're not a storefront." Gina couldn't help considering the marketing possibilities.

"No." He looked like he already had an idea.

She considered what that idea might be. "You'll need contracts with local retailers and grocery stores."

"That's the general plan." He glanced down at the table. "It's stage two. Stage one was testing the products."

"They so passed." Gina felt a shimmer of excitement. "Can I help out?"

Rafe looked surprised by the offer.

"I could talk to Lila, get a chamber directory, start making some calls."

Quenching their thirst with sparkling water, Rafe and Gina stepped out on the deck where the evening breeze was beginning to cool the concrete. He wondered if she'd stay long enough to have some wine. He'd love to sit back on the outdoor love seat and watch the sunset with her by his side.

Rafe watched her walk to the rail and gaze out at the trees, the lush valley, all the way to the mountains where the sun would set in another hour. Her hair was loose over her bare shoulders, her dress pressing gently against her thighs. While her legs, her *long, sexy legs*, took him back to that explosive night in his office…

He opened his mouth to ask her to stay, but her phone jangled from the kitchen.

She turned from the rail and smiled at him as she passed.

His stomach sank in disappointment.

It was probably something important, *someone* important. Her family, her social circle and her business network were chock-full of important people.

He polished off his water and followed her back inside, feeling like he was leaving a fantasy behind him on the deck.

"Wait," she was saying. "Slow down." She looked at Rafe with amazement in her eyes.

She had his attention.

"I don't know if I can do that," she said. Then she covered the mouthpiece and whispered, "It's Matias."

"What?" Rafe whispered back, worried.

"How—" She stopped talking for a minute. "That would be unethical."

"What?" Rafe repeated, moving closer, ready to take the phone from her hand and ask his brother what the heck was going on.

Gina held up her hand to stop him. Then she made a one-minute sign with her index finger. "Seriously, you...*seriously*?" She put her hand to her forehead in a gesture of disbelief. "Okay. Yes."

"What on earth?" Rafe didn't even bother whispering this time. He couldn't for the life of him figure out what his brother would want with Gina, but it didn't sound good.

Gina gave him the wait-one-minute hand signal again, and Rafe sucked in a frustrated breath. "I said yes. I will." She paused. "As soon as I can." Another pause. "Okay, go!" She laughed then and ended the call.

"What was *that*?" Rafe demanded.

"It was Matias." She chuckled again, gazing at her phone.

"And what, *exactly*, did my brother want from you?" Rafe had never spoken to Matias about his attraction to Gina. He'd never spoken to anyone about it. But he couldn't bring himself to believe Gina would make love with Rafe and then…he didn't know what to call it… *chat* with Matias.

"He's with Anastasia."

"Who?"

Gina gave Rafe a baffled look. "His cowboy experience person."

"Oh. Is that today?"

"Yes."

"Is something wrong?" Rafe wondered if Matias had rudely asked the woman from Boston her age. Rafe had put his money on sixty-seven, while his brother Diego was the next closest at fifty-nine. Rafe still figured he had a good shot at taking the pot.

"No. Quite the opposite." Gina typed something into her phone.

"What are you doing?"

"It's a little embarrassing."

Rafe's guard went up again. "Embarrassing how?"

"He wants me to change her ticket. Reservations, please," Gina said into the phone.

It took Rafe a minute to process the sentence.

"Hi. I'd like to change a ticket if that's possible."

"Her *plane ticket*?" Rafe asked, earning himself the wait signal yet again.

"It's for tomorrow," Gina continued. "The name on the ticket is Anastasia Kovell, but the booking was made by the Edmond Organization." Gina looked to Rafe and moved the phone under her chin.

"How old is this woman?"

Looking puzzled by his question, Gina went back to the call. "Sure. Thursday will work. It's a direct flight?" She listened. "Yes, that's right. By text is fine. Thanks very much." She ended the call.

Rafe stared at her in silence for a moment as the questions piled up inside his head.

"It seems your brother is having a good time," she said.

"With *Anastasia*?" Rafe couldn't erase the original gray-haired image of the woman from his mind.

"They're at RCW right now, probably ordering cocktails before the appetizers. It sounds like your brother wants dinner to last as long as possible."

Rafe pointed to Gina's phone. "Did you just—"

"Put my ethics on hold to buy your brother some extra time with Anastasia? Yes. I'm not proud of it, but he assured me she had the rest of the week free."

"Well, well, well." Rafe took out his own phone and texted Matias, demanding a photo.

"Rafe, wait—"

Rafe hit Send and looked up at Gina.

"Now he knows we're together."

Rafe didn't see the problem. "So?"

"He might think we're *together*, together."

Rafe wasn't crazy about the implications of her concern. Did he embarrass her? "He won't. And even if he does, we have a perfect cover story."

She lifted her palms in a gesture of incomprehension.

"It's business. You're helping me with the new bakery line."

Her phone pinged, distracting her. "It's the new ticket."

While she keyed something in on her screen, Rafe's phone pinged, too.

Matias had sent a photo, no questions asked, of a beautiful blonde woman with wide blue eyes and a dazzling smile.

"Ahhh," Rafe said aloud.

"What?" Gina moved to his side, leaning her shoulder into his arm for a better view. "Oh. *Ahhh*. Well, that explains it." She tipped her head to Rafe, her eyes alight with humor. "I just texted her that her flight was rescheduled. I feel like your partner in crime."

Her bare shoulder was warm against his skin, her gaze riveting, her lips pink and slightly parted.

His voice turned husky as he spoke. "Let's crime away." He set his phone deliberately down on the table. Then he slipped hers from her hand and set it aside. He smoothed her thick hair back, cradled her face and slowly lowered his lips to hers.

As they finally kissed, his entire being sighed in pleasure and relief.

She turned, and he wrapped his arms around her, molding her slender body to his. "This," he whispered on a rasp of emotion, kissing her again. "This is what I need."

As she opened to his kisses, one thought crowded his brain. *His bed.* He needed her in his bed, naked against him, her limbs wrapped around him.

He lifted her into his arms. His hormones surging, she felt light as a feather. His bedroom was down a hallway. He knew the way blindfolded, so he kept kissing her as they passed through the family room, around the corner, down to the end and through a set of double doors.

The screened windows were open, a fresh breeze wafting through. The setting sun cast long shadows, softening the light as he set her on her feet next to his king-size bed.

Her fingers raked his short hair, and he let his hands

roam the curve of her waist, the flare of her hips, the sides of her silken thighs.

"I've thought of you in here," he confessed.

"Nice room," she said, her gaze staying fixed on his.

"It's not exactly a palace." He almost said, "Princess."

She gave a little smile. "Who cares?"

He stripped off his shirt.

She leaned forward and kissed his chest. Her hands moved over him, exploring the contours of his shoulders and pecs, sending little shock waves of pleasure darting under his skin.

"Oh, man." He exhaled.

Her touches moved lower and lower still until he sucked in a breath.

Then she took a step back, reached behind her head, bringing her breasts to prominence against the fabric of her dress. The dress pooled at her feet, revealing a dusty blue bra and panties trimmed with lace.

He took her hands, giving in to an impulse to draw them aside, away from her body, to improve his view. "Oh, Gina."

For a moment he was too transfixed to move. He wanted to hang on to the moment. But then she freed her hands and reached for his jeans, popping the button, drawing down the zipper, igniting passion stronger than any he'd ever felt.

He shucked the rest of his clothes and drew her down on the bed. He wanted her naked, to feel her skin to skin, but couldn't give up the sexy lace.

He skimmed the smooth silk of her bra, kissed her mouth and her neck, nudged the pretty strap from her shoulder and kissed her there, too. Then he peeled off her bra and kissed her breasts. Her head tipped and her back arched and she moaned his name.

His passion crackled like a storm cloud breaking open in the sky. He hooked his thumbs under her panties and drew them down the length of her legs. He reached for the bedside drawer, then settled between her legs, reveling in her hands as they kneaded his back, moving lower, drawing him to her.

He pulled away to drink in her beauty, cradled her face in his hands, smiled at the flush of her cheeks and the swell of her bottom lip. He kissed her sweetness, drawing out the moment.

Then her hips tilted, legs wrapping around him, and with the barest of movements, they were one. He held still for as long as he could, but then she shifted and arched, and he moved with her, filling his heart and his mind with mindless pleasure.

Holding still was impossible. Slowing was impossible. A primal need drove his movements, sweat glistening on his skin, his lungs filling with oxygen, and his heart pumping furiously to keep up with his demands.

Gina's breath came in sweet puffs against his face. Her fingernails dug into his shoulders. And her legs held him locked tight as he moved to a new plane of life.

"Rafe!" she cried out, and a shudder ran through her.

He followed her over, hot and gasping, closing his eyes to drink in every last ounce of bliss. Then he held her close, kissed her hairline, her temple, her mouth.

As his breathing steadied, he rolled, easing her over on top of him, worried his weight would be uncomfortable.

She lifted her head, still breathless, and blinked down at him. "Hi."

He grinned. "Hi."

"So…" She looked uncertain.

"*Together*, together," he said. There was no question about it.

"Good thing we have a cover story."

Rafe didn't want a cover story. He wanted to shout it to the world. But he'd do whatever she wanted. So he smiled and tucked her hair behind her ears. "I won't tell if you don't."

"Deal," she whispered. A moment later she was sliding off to the side.

He wanted to hold her, stop her from leaving, but it wasn't his choice. He forced himself to keep his hands still.

But she didn't leave. Instead, she snuggled up next to him, tucking her head in the crook of his arm.

He smiled in deep satisfaction and settled into the most amazing fantasy.

Nine

Gina was dozing off in Rafe's arms when a sudden thought hit her.

"Oh, no." She sat straight up.

Rafe sat up with her. "What?"

"I forgot about the hotel." She swung her legs over the edge of the bed. "I need to extend Anastasia's stay at the Bellamy."

Rafe's forearm suddenly looped around her waist, holding her back.

"Hey," she protested.

"Let Matias worry about the hotel."

Gina shook her head. "I made it sound like the airline had canceled the flight. That means the Edmond Organization is responsible for her delay."

"I don't know how you figure that." Rafe gave a tug and pulled her onto her back on the soft bed, her head landing on a plump pillow. "This is Matias's master plan."

"But we're his collaborators. That comes with a certain responsibility."

"Fair point." His gaze seemed to drink her in. "But I *really* don't want to let you go."

"I'll come back. I will. I just need my phone."

He leaned slowly down, barely brushing his lips against hers.

Her stomach contracted. The insubstantial touch seemed somehow sexier than the lovemaking. And she'd have bet there was nothing in the world sexier than Rafe's lovemaking.

"Promise?" His whisper was a vibration.

"Promise."

"Okay." He sat up, then stood.

"You don't have to come with me." She wondered if she should put her dress on for the walk to the kitchen, but that seemed silly if she was coming straight back.

"I'll get your phone," he said, starting for the bedroom door.

"You will?" she asked, pleasantly surprised by his chivalry.

He waved at her behind his back. "Lie back down."

"Are you that afraid I won't come back?" she called in a teasing tone.

"No. I'm a gentleman." His voice echoed along the hall.

Smiling to herself, she resettled herself on the bed, drawing the sheet up over herself and gazing around Rafe's bedroom. The white leather headboard highlighted a rock feature wall bracketed by two windows. A pair of steel-blue leather armchairs shared an ottoman and sat on a cream, taupe and pale blue mottled rug. There was a large oil painting on an eggshell wall, a ranch scene, the Cortez-Williams Ranch—she recognized the old cabin and the windmill. In the opposite corner was a huge plant pot with several different species around a miniature palm.

Rafe returned and tossed her phone to her on the comforter.

"Did you decorate this yourself?" she asked as she picked it up.

"Yeah." He looked around. "Why? Do you like it?"

"It's nicely coordinated."

He climbed in next to her on the bed, pulling the sheet to his waist. "I don't strike you as coordinated?"

She took in the square-shaded wall lights on either side of the bed and the sleek-lined bedside tables. "This doesn't strike me as a rancher's design."

"What, you expected a set of longhorns over the bed?" He didn't seem annoyed, merely curious.

"Something like that."

"I bought it out of a showroom," he said.

She didn't understand.

"I went into Willenberg's downtown, saw this setup in the showroom and said I'd take the whole thing. Except for the painting. I commissioned the painting."

"I recognize it." She looked down at her phone, seeing a text message from Anastasia. "She doesn't seem upset."

"Who?" Rafe was focused on his own phone now.

"Anastasia. She's taking the delay in stride."

"Lucky Matias."

Gina smiled to herself. She could easily imagine the strapping, handsome Matias had something to do with Anastasia's blasé reaction.

She pulled up the hotel website, entering the Edmond account and password. With a few taps she'd extended the reservation two more nights. Then she forwarded the information to Anastasia.

When she set down her phone, Rafe was still working away. She watched him for a few minutes, the focus and concentration on his face. "Are you a workaholic?"

He glanced to her. "You're the one who insisted we get our phones."

"I'm done. You're still working."

"I let JJ know I loved the baking. He's excited to get started."

"That's all?" She didn't believe him.

"A couple other things, too."

"Ha! Caught. Workaholic."

"You know you're never really off the clock when you own your own business."

Gina didn't know that. She probably should have known that. She wondered if her brothers felt that way. The oil business was definitely all-consuming for her father, that was for sure.

"What are you thinking?" Rafe asked. He was looking at her now.

"It makes sense," she said. "That you'd never truly forget about work."

"Does that upset you?" He waved his phone like he was offering to put it down.

"Oh, no. It's not that."

"Then what?"

"It makes me wonder, is all." What it would be like to be needed at the office, to not have unlimited time for tennis dates or riding or lunching at the Cattleman's Club.

"About?"

"My own job."

He set his phone on the bedside table and slid down in the bed. "Tell me about it."

She was embarrassed.

"A vanity position?" he gently asked.

She nodded. "I never really worried about it. I mean, who wouldn't love a big office, an expense account and little responsibility? I can attend any meeting, read any report, I just—"

"Can't have any impact?"

She shook her head. "Exactly."

"Then they're wasting a valuable resource. I saw how you managed the auction. You could apply those skills to anything you wanted."

She wasn't so sure she could apply herself to the Edmond Organization. "There's already Rusty and Ross and Asher. They even listened to the things Billy had to say, but not me."

"Have you ever tried?"

"A few times. When I first got back from college. I'd learned some things, you know. I had some opinions."

He leaned his shoulder against hers, touched the side of his head to hers. "Nobody listened."

"Nobody listened. Are you pitying me?"

"I'm mocking you, Princess."

That wasn't the answer she'd expected. "What? Why?"

"Because it's your own fault."

She picked up the nearest pillow and bopped him in the stomach.

He laughed. "You're a member of the family, every bit as much as Ross or Asher."

"I can't force them to listen to me."

"You can try."

Gina put an exaggerated pout on her face.

He kissed her.

"Hey."

"That wasn't more mocking. It was just for fun."

She couldn't exactly argue with that. Kissing Rafe was a whole lot of fun.

"What would you do?" he asked.

"In the oil business?"

"Yes."

She did have one idea. It was something she'd wanted to bring up to Rusty for a while now. "Methane."

Rafe's brow went up.

"There are whole new ways to capture the off-gas methane from oil wells and convert it to energy—heat, even electrical. It protects the environment and provides a reduced-cost source of energy for the oil field operation."

He looked surprised. "Have you ever suggested it?"

She shook her head. "They won't even listen to my marketing ideas, never mind something operational."

He seemed to ponder. "Tie the idea to marketing."

"How?"

"I don't know. It's environmentally friendly—corporate reputation, maybe."

Gina's brain lit up with the suggestion. She came to her knees and faced him, ideas forming one after the other. She grinned. "I can do something with that."

"Good," he said.

"You're smart."

"You're sexy."

"You're off topic."

"No." He reached for her. "I'm exactly *on* topic."

His touch was distracting, his kisses more so, and it was only seconds before she was succumbing to the luxury of his embrace.

Rafe expected Gina to forget about her offer of help with Royal Chamber of Commerce contacts. She'd been excited about pressing her family on the methane technology, and he knew she was already busy with planning her mother's wedding. But even without her, RCW was pressing forward on his own.

They didn't want to spend a lot of money on the bakery launch, since that would defeat the whole purpose. But the staff members had enthusiastically stepped up to help control costs.

Janelle, one of the hostesses, was studying graphic art and had mocked up a logo, while Samuel's father had a wholesale line on display baskets. JJ's mother had taken a no-nonsense approach to sizing up the kitchen and planning supplies, while virtually everyone had volunteered to help package the sample baking baskets. All that was left to Rafe was to find the right contacts and deliver sample baskets in the hopes of getting them to agree to sell the baking products.

He was about to call Lila when JJ rapped twice and opened the office door.

"What's up?" Rafe asked from behind his desk.

"It's Matias. He's in the dining room."

"Is he looking for me?"

JJ shook his head. "He's with a gorgeous woman. So far, he's looking for two April Rain martinis."

Rafe immediately rose, curious to meet the woman, who had to be Anastasia.

"If you're doing a recon, report back," JJ said.

"Will do," Rafe said as he cut through the kitchen.

The couple was at a round table in a corner of the main dining room, a mini hurricane lamp flickering in the center of the white tablecloth.

Rafe smoothly approached, keeping his voice low and conversational. "Hi, Matias."

Matias didn't seem surprised to see him. "Anastasia, this is my brother Rafe."

Rafe turned his attention to the woman, offering his hand.

She was stunningly beautiful, with porcelain pale skin, bright blue eyes and long platinum blond hair. Her smile revealed perfect white teeth as she accepted his hand.

"Hello, Rafe." Her fingers were long and slender, with a delicate emerald ring on her right hand. It matched her stud earrings and a small pendant that hung above the neckline of her peach-toned dress. Everything about her said class and dignity, even her smooth, gentle voice. "Matias told me about you."

"Nothing bad, I hope."

"All good. He promised I'd love RCW, and I do."

Rafe looked at his brother, who gave him a beaming smile that clearly asked if Anastasia was not the most amazing woman on earth. Rafe had to respectfully disagree; beautiful as she was, Gina had her beat. But he could see why Matias had wanted to keep Anastasia around for a while longer.

"You're from Boston?" Rafe asked her, detecting only a slight accent.

"Born and raised, in Brookline to be precise."

"And you bid on this mangy cowboy?" She struck

Rafe as much too refined for the daylong horseback riding adventure Matias had offered up.

"I've always been a rebel."

"Did you ride in Boston?"

"Some, English style mostly, but it translates."

"It translates perfectly," Matias said and reached across the table for her hand, his eyes glowing.

The waitress arrived with their lime-garnished glasses and frosted martini shakers, and Rafe moved to get out of the way. "Enjoy your meal."

"Thank you," Anastasia said.

"Can you stop by later?" Matias asked.

"Sure. No problem." Rafe was a little surprised Matias would want another interruption in his evening.

As he made his way through the dining room, he stopped at a few tables to welcome the guests and ask how they were enjoying their meals.

Laughing with one family foursome, he glanced up to see Gina standing in the entry lobby. His heart lifted at the sight of her, and he quickly wrapped up the conversation.

She watched as he rounded the last few tables, smiling as he approached.

"Hi," she said.

"Hi, yourself." He was ridiculously glad to see her.

"I made some calls," she told him. "I got a contact list from the chamber and reached out to grocery retailers. They're all excited about the new product line."

"You did all that?" He was stunned.

Now she looked puzzled. "I said I would."

"I know, but that was only Monday, and you've got other things on the go."

"Other things?"

"Your work for Edmond, your mother's wedding."

"I can multitask. And you'll be happy to know my bridesmaid dress still fits even after all those baking samples."

He brought up the fond memory. "Well, that's probably because we—" Rafe stopped himself before he could finish the sentence. He also had to stop himself from brushing back her hair, reminding himself they were standing in a crowd. "Come back to the office."

"Okay."

He wanted to take her hand, but instead he simply led the way, cutting through the corner of the kitchen to the quiet and privacy of his office.

As he shut the door, her gaze went to his desk and lingered there for a second. He hoped she was remembering their lovemaking. He'd never forget the feel of her body around his that night.

He gestured to the armchair grouping beside the window. "Can I get you anything to drink? A cocktail or perhaps a glass of wine?"

"Glass of wine, sure."

She sat down and crossed her long legs beneath her tidy steel blue dress as he called the front desk and asked for a bottle of his favorite merlot and two glasses. Then he joined her, sitting across the low coffee table.

"I've made a spreadsheet." She set a couple of pages in front of him. "It's got the business name, owner, manager and purchasing contact, phone number, email address, and a short description of their initial reaction to the pitch."

"You made a pitch?"

"I just reworded some of the stuff you said while we

were sampling, plus a few of my own impressions of the quality to personalize it."

Rafe gazed at the pages in disbelief. "You did all this? For *me*?"

"I thought that was what we agreed?" She sounded worried, like maybe she'd done something wrong.

"Yes, yes, it was. I'm just astounded that you did such a great job."

"Don't start sounding like my family." There was a thread of annoyance in her voice.

He looked up at her. "What?"

"Don't act surprised that I can tie my shoes."

"Tie your *shoes*?"

"Correctly complete rudimentary tasks."

"*This* isn't a rudimentary task. It's fantastic. It's perfect. We've been working on sample baskets, a logo, and now you—" He gave his head a little shake, telling himself to stop rattling on and get to his point. "This is *exactly* what we needed. Thank you." He rose to give her a kiss of appreciation.

When he drew back, she looked guarded, and he feared he'd been too presumptuous with the kiss. Before she could ask, a knock came on the door.

It was Janelle with the wine and glasses on a tray.

Rafe invited her in, feeling honor bound to share her contribution with Gina.

"Janelle designed a logo for us," he told Gina as the young woman set up the glasses and opened the bottle.

"I'm using it as credit for a college course I'm taking." Janelle deftly pulled the cork, allowing the wine to breathe for a few minutes. Meanwhile, he brought up the logo on his laptop. His hostess had used the same basic elements as RCW but replaced the R for Rafe with a Y for Yeoh, creating the Yeoh-Cortez-Williams YCW Sweethouse brand. "Come take a look."

Both Gina and Janelle joined him at the screen.

"That's incredible," Gina said, smiling at Janelle. "You are so talented."

"Thanks. But I really can't take all the credit. Rafe came up with the YCW idea, and Mrs. Yeoh suggested Sweethouse as a play on Steakhouse."

"This is totally going to work," Gina said with conviction.

"I couldn't agree more," Janelle replied. "And I can't wait for us to get going on this!"

Rafe would have preferred to get going on the bottle of wine with Gina, but he knew better than to interrupt this level of enthusiasm.

Squaring her shoulders, Gina marched into her father's Edmond Organization office, determined to force him to listen. Behind his big desk he was glaring at his computer screen, a deep scowl on his face.

"This is ridiculous!" he ground out before she could say a thing.

She was used to his outbursts, and it was usually best not to probe for details. "Dad, I have something important to—"

"Have you seen it?" he asked, voice elevated, eyes smoldering with rage.

"Seen what?"

He spun his screen. "Today, yesterday, the day before. *That liar just won't stop.*"

Gina scanned over a list of social media posts that had thousands of reactions and responses. Billy was still out there ranting about Rusty's dishonesty, about

Ross's disloyalty, about Asher not even being a real Edmond and all about how unfair his life was now and had always been. There were also posts that said the Edmonds owed him everything, and he was going to get revenge on them all.

She'd seen some of these rants before, but it was definitely getting worse. "Can the police not track him down?"

Rusty's eyes were still ablaze. "You don't think I've *asked*?"

"So they can't." She realized this was a bad time to propose her business idea. Her father wasn't about to say yes to anything in this state.

Ross came into the office, focused on his cell phone screen, this thumb scrolling. "What about another private investigator?" He looked at Gina. "Did you read these?"

"Just now," she answered. "I don't understand how he can be that active and still stay hidden."

"He's smart enough to ping through a whole raft of countries. We should try a bigger firm," Ross said to Rusty. "Maybe go international. He could be in Mexico or Canada, or may have even chartered a jet overseas. He's probably got money hidden around the world."

"Yes!" Rusty said to Ross. "Do it now. I want this over and done with."

Gina wasn't convinced that finding Billy would end anything. Sure, the rat could end up in jail, and they might even get some of the money back. But fissures in the family had been revealed through Billy's crimes, and it was going to take them a very long time to recover from those.

And when they did, the family dynamics were going

to be different. Rusty and Ross and Asher didn't know it yet, but she intended to be an active participant in running the Edmond Organization. She had an equal ownership position with her two brothers, and she wasn't going to sit on the sidelines and play nice anymore.

"I'll set it up," Ross said and turned to go.

Gina took the opportunity to follow him out the door into the executive reception area, out of the line of Rusty's fire. "Can I talk to you?"

"Sure," Ross said, tucking his phone away. "About the wedding?"

"No."

He looked puzzled. "Oh. I thought you and Mom were working on that."

"We are, and it's coming together."

"I hope so, since it's a week from Saturday."

"You did the tux fitting?" She followed him into his office.

"I did. I'll be perfectly dressed to escort Mom down the aisle. I heard you picked a cake."

"We did. The cake is going to be incredible." She shut the door behind herself. "But that's not why I'm here."

"Oh?" He took a seat at a table for four and pushed a stack of reports out of the way.

Gina sat next to him and turned her chair to better face him. "Ross."

He looked intently at her. "Gina."

"You know I work here, right?"

"Well, you have an office right across the hall, an expense account and we pay you every month. So, yeah, I know you work here."

"I want to *really* work here. And I have an idea…"

He looked a little wary. "Okay."

"Don't look like that."

"Like what?" he asked.

"You haven't even heard it yet."

He gave a shrug, but his phone buzzed in his pocket, and he glanced down. His expression told her she was already losing his attention.

"Tell me your idea," he said, reaching for the phone.

Her hand shot forward, stopping him from reaching into his pocket. "I want you to listen."

He let his hand drop. "Okay. I'm listening."

"Methane," she said.

"What about it?"

"You know there are new technologies out there, right? Techniques to capture methane from the wells and generate energy."

"I do know that."

"Good. I've been looking at ways we can make use of the methane energy for our field operations."

Ross blinked silently.

"I've written a report. It's good. It's solid. And I want your support when I take it to Dad."

It took Ross a moment longer to speak. "You're writing a report on the utilization of methane power conversion technologies for Edmond?"

"Exactly."

"You have an engineering degree I don't know about?"

"I can read, Ross. I talk to experts. I can understand complex systems."

He furrowed his brow. "Exactly what does this have to do with marketing? You are still in the marketing department, right?"

"Don't be condescending."

He held up his palms in surrender as his phone buzzed again.

"Don't touch that," she warned.

"Wouldn't dream of it."

"In two years, five years, ten years…it's going to matter. Dad might not be thinking of it right now, but oil companies that are more environmentally friendly are going to have an advantage in the future with both shareholders and customers for starters. Plus, it's the right thing to do, and ultimately, it will save us money."

"It's a miracle?" he asked with an edge of sarcasm.

"No. It's good technology and smart business."

His phone buzzed again.

"Gina," he said, pointing to the phone. "It might be important."

"*This* is important. All I want is your support. If I can't make the case, I can't make the case. But I need Dad and you and Asher to give it a fair look, a serious look. Just don't blow me off this time."

"We don't—"

"*Yes*, you do. You always have. I open my mouth in a meeting, and everyone goes for their phones." She looked pointedly at his pocket.

"Okay," he finally said. "Okay. I promise I'll give it a fair read."

"And?" she prompted.

"And I'll support you with Dad."

She couldn't help but smile in both relief and gratitude.

"*Now* can I answer my cell?"

"Yes. Thanks, Ross." Her heart lifted with hope as she left his office.

Ten

Despite everything that had happened between them, Rafe felt awkward calling Gina for what was essentially a date. It was impossible to pin a description on their relationship, impossible to even *call* it a relationship, even though he would be her escort to her mother's wedding.

He did have a good excuse for this particular invitation, and it was more of a double date really. Staring at his phone, he decided he was probably overthinking this. He pulled her number from his contact list and placed the call.

"Rafe?" She didn't sound elated to hear from him. But she didn't sound annoyed, either. She sounded more puzzled than anything.

"Hi," he said, ridiculously happy to hear her voice.

"Hi. What's going on?" The background sound said she was on the move.

"Where are you?"

"On my way into the Edmond building, why?"

Rafe glanced at his watch to confirm it was barely nine. "On a Sunday morning?"

"I'm working on something."

"Yeah?" He was interested.

"Polishing up the methane proposal."

"You got right on that."

"I already had a bunch of the information indexed. And the industry contacts have been fantastic. They're really excited about their recent tech progress."

"I'm glad to hear that, Gina."

"It's going well." She sounded satisfied.

The background sounds changed, and he knew she was inside.

"Can you take a little time off?" he asked.

"When? Why?"

"Tonight. Matias wants me to have dinner with him and Anastasia, and I thought—"

"Anastasia's still in Royal?"

"Yes."

"But her ticket to Boston was for Thursday."

"She's still here. I suggested you—"

"I didn't change it." Gina was clearly baffled.

"Maybe Anastasia changed it."

"On the Edmond account?" she asked. "How would she do that?"

"Maybe she missed the flight. Maybe Matias bought her a new ticket."

"But that would be—"

"*Gina.* The plane ticket is not the point."

"And what is the point?"

"I suggested Anastasia might like to meet you, too."

She didn't respond.

"Tonight," Rafe said. "With me. At dinner."

There was another beat of silence. "I can't believe she's stayed this long."

"That's not an answer. Dinner?"

"Yes. Sure. Of course. I can wrap things up here whenever you like."

Rafe liked her reaction—a lot. Like it was no big deal and a foregone conclusion that they could casually do a dinner together.

"Can I pick you up at seven?"

"I should change."

"I meant from your house."

"Oh." There was a clear hesitation in her voice.

"Is that a problem?" Was she reluctant to have him show up at the Edmond home?

"No." She quickly backtracked. "Not a problem. I'll be ready."

Rafe ordered himself to quit scrutinizing his relationship with Gina, to quit looking for pitfalls. They might not have talked about themselves as a couple, and so far, they'd kept their personal life a secret. But she'd agreed to come out with him tonight. Sure, curiosity about Anastasia had to be part of the draw. But she was coming out as his *date*.

He was slightly early pulling into the ridiculously expensive tiled roundabout at the Elegance Ranch. Without the crowds this time, the place was beyond imposing. Its multistory peaked roof rose to the sky, while marble pillars bracketed two oversize glass-adorned front doors. It boasted huge bay windows on either side of the wide porch, with balconies above on the second floor overlooking the sweeping majesty of the front lawn.

He left his SUV in front, expecting to be in and out quickly.

His ring of the bell was answered by a neatly suited middle-aged man, obviously a staff member.

"May I help you, sir?"

Rafe was glad to be well dressed himself in a favorite steel-gray suit with a pressed white shirt and a burgundy tie. People didn't look down on him when he was dressed like this. "I'm here for Gina."

The older man moved back and widened the doorway. "Please come in."

"Thank you." Rafe stepped onto the gleaming marble floor for a second time. It was hushed inside today. The decor was impeccable, the airy hall spotless, and the two wrought iron railed staircases were impressively glorious. The Edmonds sure knew how to build an entrance.

"Your name, sir?"

"Rafe Cortez-Williams."

"I'll let Ms. Edmond know you've arrived. Feel free to wait here, or in the library if you'd be more comfortable."

"I'm fine here."

As the man disappeared up the stairs, Ross appeared at the far side of the hall, coming around the corner from what Rafe knew was the great room. He had a heavy-bottomed highball glass in his hand, half full of something amber. Rafe guessed bourbon but possibly whiskey or a single-malt scotch.

"Hey, Rafe." Ross walked forward. The curiosity

in his eyes told him Gina hadn't talked to her family about their date.

"Hi," he answered.

Ross came to a halt. "You're here to…"

"Auction follow-up," Rafe said, in case Gina wanted to continue being completely circumspect. "We're having dinner with one of the winning bidders."

"You and Gina?"

"Yes."

The man's gaze narrowed for a second. He took a contemplative sip of his drink. "So, you gave up your Chamber of Commerce funding."

"I did."

"That's a lot of money. Any particular reason?"

Rafe tried to figure out where Ross was going with this. "Valencia will make good use of it."

"Simple as that?" Ross's skepticism was clear.

"Simple as—" Before Rafe could finish speaking, Gina appeared on the staircase, and his breath was momentarily taken away.

Her dress was shimmering black, a halter top with a beaded V-neck that showed off her shoulders and dipped between her breasts. It was snug over her slim waist, while the skirt was full and flirty. But the part that practically left him gasping was the bright red satin lining visible under the asymmetrical hemline.

Her shoes were black, too, open-toed with a crisscross around her ankle and red sole that flashed as she walked. Sexy didn't begin to describe the outfit.

"Where exactly are you guys going?" Ross asked, taking another sip of his drink.

"The Bellamy," Rafe answered, his gaze not leaving Gina.

She smiled as she stepped off the staircase, and his chest went tight in reaction.

"The restaurant, right?" Ross asked.

"Very funny," Gina said, making a face at her brother. "We're meeting Matias and his auction purchaser. She's from Boston."

"Trying to impress the big-city folk?" Ross asked, taking in her outfit.

"Exactly," Gina answered. Then she linked her arm with Rafe's. "Ready?"

"Absolutely. Bye, Ross." They turned for the door, and Rafe could feel the other man's speculative gaze on him as they left.

"You look fantastic," Rafe said as he opened the SUV door for her.

She had to grip the handle and step on the running board to get into the high vehicle. For a moment he wished he had a sports car instead. Gina would look *incredible* in a Porsche.

"You okay?" he asked as she got settled.

She looked confused. "Fine, why?"

"The seat's a little high."

She waved away his concern. "Don't let the outfit throw you off. You know I'm a perfectly capable woman."

He couldn't help but grin. "I know that very well."

Gina immediately liked Anastasia.

They'd been seated at a white-draped table with a pretty flower centerpiece near the atrium and with a view of the gardens. Ballerina-thin, Anastasia wore a dusty-rose dress with a beaded mesh bodice, spaghetti straps over her creamy shoulders and a full chiffon skirt that accentuated her shapely legs.

When they'd walked in, her movements were smoothly graceful.

"Do you dance?" Gina asked her after they'd ordered cocktails.

"Ballet when I was a girl."

"I took a little ballet," Gina said. "Switched to modern pretty early."

"My parents were traditionalists. Classical ballet three times a week."

"You must be good."

She gave a little shrug. "It was more for them than me."

"Ahhh, parents."

"Yes." Anastasia's gaze wandered to Matias, who was talking with Rafe.

"You must like it here in Royal," Gina ventured, probing for a little information.

"I know you were part of the plot to keep me here."

"I…" She was embarrassed to be called out.

But Anastasia laughed. "Don't worry. I don't mind that Matias was a little crafty, and I admire that you and Rafe supported his brother."

Gina didn't know what to say to that.

"I'm an only child," Anastasia explained. "I always wanted siblings. They would have been a friend, and would have taken some of the parental intensity off me. Do you have brothers or sisters?"

"Two brothers. One's a stepbrother."

"It must be nice."

"It has its moments." Gina thought back to Ross's pledge of support with the methane report. But then there was the falling-out between Ross and Rusty over Ross's wife, Charlotte, the fact that Asher was arrested and that the family had doubted him, and Billy, who it seemed increasingly likely was Rusty's illegitimate son.

"There's discord, too," Gina was quick to add. "Don't let anybody tell you big families are happy families."

Anastasia nodded to Matias and Rafe, who were now chuckling about something. "To be honest, that there is what I picture in a big family."

"That's the best of it," Gina agreed, contemplating Rafe's relationship with Matias and Lorenzo. She thought back to the Sunday barbecue when they'd taken the auction pictures. The Cortez-Williams family seemed very close-knit, incredibly fun-loving and loyal.

Rafe saw them looking over and quickly included them in the conversation. "Anastasia, Matias tells me your father teaches at Harvard?"

Anastasia looked uncomfortable for a moment and hesitated over her answer. "It's more of an affiliation than an actual job. He does have a doctorate from Harvard, but he's not a teaching professor."

"Oh," Rafe asked conversationally. "What does he do?"

"He sits on a few boards." She paused. "Makes a few donations."

Matias seemed surprised. "I thought—"

"Any area in particular?" Gina asked, hoping Rafe's question hadn't inadvertently caused friction between the two.

Anastasia looked at Matias. "It's not on the Harvard campus, per se. It's a fine arts pavilion." An apology came into her eyes. "The Kovell Fine Arts Pavilion."

"Wait," Matias said.

"And Academy," she finished, cringing slightly.

Gina recognized the name of the institution. It was prestigious and huge, and owned by...

Matias was shaking his head now. Luckily the drinks arrived, because he looked like he could use one. He took a swallow of his martini as the waitress left.

"You really are slumming," he said to Anastasia.

"No. I'm *rebelling.*"

"And that's different how?" Matias was clearly annoyed.

Gina looked to Rafe, thinking maybe they should leave for a minute and give the couple some privacy.

Rafe started to rise. "Gina and I will—"

"No," Matias said. His smile was brittle. "No. It's not the end of the world. She was only supposed to be in Texas for two days. We've had five. I'm grateful for that." He raised his glass. "Thank you, Anastasia, for buying me and for coming all the way to Royal for an experience."

"Matias..." she said.

He rocked his glass meaningfully, annoyance still in his eyes.

Gina quickly raised her Bordeaux, hoping to help defuse the situation and give Rafe's brother a moment to calm down. "Welcome to Royal, Anastasia."

"Hear, hear." Rafe raised his glass as well.

Looking none too happy, Anastasia joined the toast.

Afterward, she was quiet for a moment.

Gina searched her mind for a safe topic.

But Anastasia spoke up. "I'm not going back there."

All three of them looked at her.

"I like it here," she said airily. "And I'm staying. Date me if you want to, Matias. Dump me if you want to.

But I'm sticking around. Maybe I'll buy some real estate." She turned to Gina. "Do you know a good agent?"

Gina opened her mouth, not knowing what to say.

"Don't be ridiculous," Matias said.

"Matias." Rafe's tone was warning.

Matias glared at his brother.

"*What* are you doing?" Rafe demanded. Matias started to speak, but Rafe cut him off. "So she's richer than you thought. So what?"

"She—"

"Didn't tell some random auction cowboy her family had more money than royalty? Right out of the gate? I wonder why?"

Matias paused, his expression going pensive.

"I wouldn't either," Gina put in. "If I was in a new city, meeting a new guy, I wouldn't tell him about my family."

She caught Rafe's amused expression out of the corner of her eye.

"Okay," she said in response. "So, my family is pretty much infamous now. But still, you get my point. Who wants to be judged by your family? I know I don't."

"I didn't mean to keep it from you," Anastasia said to Matias. "I didn't lie, I just didn't…"

"Bring full financial statements on a first date," Rafe finished for her. "Get a grip, Matias. She's obviously way out of your league, and you're being a jerk, and she's still willing to give you a second chance. Apologize, thank her very much and order an appetizer already."

Gina almost laughed.

Anastasia tried to hide it, but she was clearly amused.

Even Matias rolled his eyes, shook his head, but then

he smiled. "Fine. I'm sorry. I don't know why I reacted that way."

A waiter, clearly one with impeccable timing, arrived with their dinner menus.

The rest of the evening passed in fine food, good drinks and a luscious crème brûlée that Gina shared with Rafe for dessert. Then they were saying a cheerful good-night and she was climbing back into Rafe's SUV.

"She seems great," Gina said, settling into the soft seat as Rafe started the vehicle.

"Matias is a lucky guy," Rafe agreed. He backed out of the parking spot and steered them toward the exit. "Tired?"

"A little, yeah. It was a fun night."

"So…what…now…?" His voice was a sexy rumble above the sound of the engine. "Do you want me to take you home?"

She turned, gazing at his profile in the strobing streetlights. "Is that what you want?"

He glanced sideways and slowly scanned his way to her toes. "What I want is to take you, those shoes and that sexy little dress straight back to my bedroom."

Her skin flushed with heat while anticipation constricted her chest. "That. Let's do that."

The day of Sarabeth's wedding, Rafe drove to Mustang Point alone. Gina had traveled there with her mother and the rest of the wedding party the night before in a private plane. He'd booked himself a room at the Trinity Grand Bayside Hotel, a short drive from the marina where the wedding yacht would be moored.

Lorenzo and Matias were also attending the wedding and planned to stay at the Grand.

Rafe checked in and pocketed his key card as his bag was whisked away by the bell captain.

"You made it." Lorenzo approached with Valencia by his side.

Rafe gave Valencia an affectionate hug. "Good drive down?" he asked them both.

"We're all checked in, nice view of the marina from our suite. We were about to have lunch. Want to join us?"

"Sounds good to me," Rafe said. "Did Matias make it yet?"

"Should be here anytime," Lorenzo said. "They flew straight into Houston."

"Flew?" It was an easy three-hour drive from Royal.

"He didn't tell you?"

"Tell me what?" Rafe had spent the past week working with JJ and Mrs. Yeoh on the baking launch—that was when he wasn't taking every spare hour to snatch a little sexy time with Gina.

"He went to Boston to meet the parents."

"*Anastasia's* parents?"

"Let's get a table," Valencia suggested. "I'm starving."

"Sure, sweetheart." Lorenzo gently touched the small of her back as the three of them started for the lobby restaurant.

They were shown to a table beside the picture windows with a view of Trinity Bay. The beach was filled with families and sunbathers. Swimmers bobbed out in the ocean and volleyball games were underway on the sand. The shouts and calls of it all were muted through the glass.

As he sat down, Rafe glimpsed the wedding party at

a table on the far side of the restaurant. Ross caught his gaze and gave him a curt nod—not a welcoming expression by any means. But Ross didn't have to worry. Rafe wasn't going to intrude on their family time.

Both Gina and Sarabeth had their backs to Rafe, while Ross's wife, Charlotte, was in profile, as were Asher and Lani.

"I see our timing is perfect," Matias said as he and Anastasia arrived.

Lorenzo quickly hopped up to move his chair closer to Valencia, making room for Matias to add a fifth seat to the round table.

"How was the visit in Boston?" Rafe asked Matias, curious about what had happened there.

"Her father hates me."

"He doesn't hate you," Anastasia quickly put in.

Out of the corner of his eye, Rafe caught sight of Zach Benning and Lila Jones being shown to a table. They were dining with Carter Crane and Abby Carmichael, obviously all here for the wedding.

"Who can blame him?" Lorenzo asked on a note of amusement, earning him a warning touch on the arm from Valencia.

His brother's fiancée liked to keep things calm. It served her well in working with horses and troubled kids, but the rowdy banter among the Cortez-Williams brothers sometimes made her uncomfortable.

Lorenzo kept on talking. "If I had a daughter of Anastasia's caliber, I'd want to keep her far away from a cowboy like you."

Even Valencia laughed at the joke and seemed to relax again.

"Mother *loved* him," Anastasia said to the group. "She'll bring Daddy around."

"I don't think a rancher was what he had in mind for his baby girl," Matias said, looking around for a waiter. "Have you guys ordered yet? I'm starving."

"Thank you, Matias," Valencia said. "Maybe we can get some appetizers to get us going?"

Rafe caught the eye of a waiter and gave a quick nod of his head. The man came straight over.

He handed menus around and offered to take drink orders.

Iced tea seemed to be everyone's preferred beverage, while Valencia and Matias agreed on a large appetizer platter with fresh guacamole.

"What do you think he had in mind for his baby girl?" Rafe asked Matias, his gaze straying to the Edmond table again, wondering if they had specific aspirations for Gina.

"Someone refined," Matias answered. "Likes the symphony and all that, maybe with a PhD in literature and wearing tweed."

Anastasia was clearly trying not to laugh at Matias's description.

"You disagree?" Rafe asked her.

She shook her head. "No, I completely agree. I've been dating guys like that since high school." She put her perfectly manicured hand on Matias's arm. "I didn't know what I was missing."

Valencia rubbed Lorenzo's shoulder. "Can't do better than a Cortez-Williams man."

Rafe looked at Gina again.

Lorenzo leaned over to give Valencia a quick kiss of appreciation.

Rafe caught a glimpse of the smiles and laughter between the two couples at Zach and Carter's table. It made sense that everyone was in a good mood anticipating tonight's wedding and the lavish reception and harbor cruise to follow.

"You're here solo?" Lorenzo asked Rafe, and it occurred to him that he'd been more than circumspect about Gina.

Rafe nodded to the far table. "I'm Gina Edmond's plus one."

Both of his brothers looked surprised. "Seriously?"

Anastasia looked confused by their reaction. "Gina came to dinner with him last weekend."

"That was business," Rafe said, sticking to their cover story. "The wedding's business, too, her cowboy experience."

Everyone looked at him in confusion.

"A bit of an inside joke," he said, wishing he'd kept his mouth shut about that. "She donated to the auction, and I agreed to be her escort to the wedding."

"This is a paying gig?" Matias joked.

Rafe shot him a reflexive glare. "The donation was to the Chamber of Commerce fund."

"Which I very much appreciated," Valencia said. "We've used the money to add three horses to the new stable and make room for ten more kids this year."

"I would have done it anyway," Rafe told Matias. He wanted to be clear on that.

"Who wouldn't?" Lorenzo joked. Then he looked at Valencia. "I mean, not me or anything."

Everyone laughed again.

"Any single guy would," Rafe said, putting a thread

of humor in his own voice. He wasn't annoyed with Matias. He was only annoyed with himself.

The waiter arrived with the iced tea and another one set the appetizer platter in the middle of the table while Rafe watched Gina's party rise to their feet. She was talking with Charlotte and smiling about something. Then her gaze caught Rafe's and he physically felt the punch.

She said something more to Charlotte, then something to her mother, then she started his way.

The two waiters finished their work just as Gina arrived at the table.

"Hi, all," she said, putting a hand on the back of Rafe's chair.

He stood.

There was a round of hellos to Gina.

"Thanks for coming," she said warmly to them all. "Nice to see you again, Anastasia."

"Anything you need?" Rafe asked her.

"Not just now." Their eyes met and held for a moment before she turned her attention back to the group. "The chaos seems to be somewhat under control. There were a few bad moments with the cake, and a minor flower emergency that we were able to resolve." She glanced at her watch. "But the afternoon is young."

They all chuckled.

She put her hand on Rafe's shoulder and looked at him again. "See you after the ceremony."

"You bet," he said, wishing with all his heart he dared to pull her into his arms.

She sent a smile all around. "See you tonight."

Rafe watched her for a moment before sitting down. Then he looked up to see everyone staring silently his way.

"What?"

"Just business?" Lorenzo asked.

"She's been helping with the bakery launch. You saw how she handled the auction. She does terrific work."

"You had a bit of dopey look on your face there," Matias said.

"Matias," Valencia admonished.

"She's a beautiful woman," Rafe said matter-of-factly, temporarily shaking off his longing. "We all agreed on that. And I get to dance with her later."

"Business doesn't get any better than that," Anastasia offered with a grin.

"Exactly." Rafe made a show of scanning the appetizer platter. "Who said they were hungry?"

Eleven

In the captain's stateroom of the *Azure Moon* yacht, Gina helped Sarabeth with her final preparations. It was thirty minutes to the ceremony and the weather and wind were both cooperating. The ceremony would be held outdoors at the bow, while the formal reception would spread out in the ballroom and the aft deck. Dinner would be on the main deck with dancing later on the lower deck and a mix-and-mingle bar outside on the upper sundeck around the pool.

This afternoon at the Grand hotel spa, she and Sarabeth had both indulged in facials, mani-pedis, and professional hair and makeup. Now the hairdresser was anchoring the pearl-and-rhinestone comb into the loose knot of Sarabeth's beautiful blond hair. She had romantic wisps around her face, sparse enough to show off her dangling diamond earrings.

Gina was wearing her favorite diamond studs and the little cluster diamond necklace her mother had bought her as a keepsake. The seafoam chiffon felt light and airy on her legs. She'd sprayed just a touch of sheen on her tanned shoulders, and her brunette hair was swept back in a simpler style than Sarabeth's.

Gina double-checked the cream-and-pale-yellow rose bouquets sitting out on the table. They were subtle and classy, with just a hint of greenery to set off the blooms. Their shoes were ready to be put on at the last minute—no point in wearing out their feet too early—although they'd both brought along dancing slippers for later in the evening.

A knock sounded on the cabin door.

Gina moved to get it while Sarabeth and the hairdresser perfected the comb's placement.

It was Ross. "Got a minute?" he asked in a low tone.

Asher was standing behind him in the narrow corridor.

"Now?" Gina whispered back.

"We need to give you a heads-up."

They both looked serious, so Gina moved into the passage and pulled the door mostly shut behind her. "What's wrong?"

"It's Billy."

"What about Billy?" Who cared about Billy Holmes twenty minutes before the wedding ceremony?

"The overseas private investigative firm sent Dad a report."

Gina rolled her eyes. "This is a Rusty emergency?" She looked back and forth between her two brothers. "You don't think Dad's just trying to mess with the wedding?"

"No. Rusty doesn't care about the wedding," Ross said.

"He doesn't want Sarabeth to be happy," Gina countered. "He doesn't want *anyone* to be happy."

Both men considered that for a second.

"True," Ross said. "But that's not what this is."

"Gina?" Sarabeth called from inside the cabin.

"Be right there, Mom," Gina called back.

"Who's out there?"

"It's just Ross and Asher."

"Tell Ross I'll be a few more minutes."

"Will do," Gina called back.

"Take your time," Ross called out.

"So, what is it?" Gina asked her brothers.

The yacht pitched a little under her feet.

"They've got a line on some of the money," Ross said. "They're following trails in the Caymans, Singapore and Belize."

"Well, that's good news." She didn't know why they'd have to warn her about that.

"It's the first significant movement in months," Asher said. "They're boxing him in, and they think he might react to it."

"He could get desperate," Ross said.

"Then maybe he'll make a mistake," she suggested.

"If he thinks the money's being threatened—"

Asher jumped in. "They think he might switch to blackmail."

Ross gave Gina a meaningful look, like he wanted her to fill in a blank. "So…"

Astonishment rose within her. "Are you asking if I can be blackmailed?"

"Can you?"

"No. What is this? Are you actually warning me to hide *the bodies*?"

"We don't know what you—"

She cut Ross off. "I can't be blackmailed, guys. There's nothing." She gave a little laugh. "No videotapes of me with married men. No hate-filled rants. No tax evasion. No criminal financial transactions."

"Good," Asher said.

"I can't believe you had to ask me."

"Gina," Ross said. "Have you been paying attention for the past year? This family has a whole crapton of secrets."

"Well, none of them are mine." She thought for a second about Rafe, but Billy could hardly blackmail her over him.

She'd admit to the world she was sleeping with Rafe before she'd pay out a dime to Billy or anyone else. She didn't care who knew about the two of them. For some reason, it had been a secret at the start, but she couldn't even remember why anymore.

The door opened behind her and Sarabeth appeared. "I'm ready," she said breathlessly.

Both men immediately smiled.

"You look wonderful, Mom," Ross said.

"You'll knock 'em dead, Sarabeth," Asher added. "I better get up there." With a wave, he headed down the corridor.

"The bouquets," Gina remembered. But behind Sarabeth, the hairdresser was already handing them over.

"You look perfect." She gave her mom a beaming smile. "I can't wait to see you come down the staircase." Then she left down the corridor like Asher.

"I guess this is it," Ross said, stepping back to look at them both. "Let's go wow the guests."

Some guests were seated, the rest clustered more casually around the edges for the short ceremony, filling the bow of the mega-yacht right to the rails. Rafe stood near the back edge of the crowd, making sure his height didn't block others from seeing the ceremony.

A curving staircase flowed down one side of the deck space. It was elegantly decorated with white roses, greenery and subtle lighting, creating a bridal pathway with the sun setting far across the bay.

The music came up and the crowd quieted as Gina appeared at the top of the staircase. She started gracefully down, a bouquet in her hands, her pale sea-blue dress caressing her thighs. Rafe's vision tunneled to her, and everything around him disappeared.

She looked happy as she took the crowd in from one end to the other. Then she spotted Rafe, and her gaze stopped moving. Her lips curved into the softest of smiles just for him. At least it felt like it was just for him.

He started to move toward her but stopped himself just in time.

She wasn't his, even if he wished with all his heart that she was.

She stepped off at the bottom of the stairs, and the music changed. Everyone's attention moved from Gina back to the top of the staircase where Sarabeth was on Ross's arm.

Rafe gave the bride a glance, but then looked back at Gina. She was by far the most beautiful woman he'd ever seen, full red lips, rosy cheeks, shiny, thick hair that glowed in the waning rays of the sun. Her bare shoulders shone, and he longed to run his hands over them. He couldn't wait for the dancing to start so he could hold her in his arms.

The ceremony was brief, and then Brett was kissing Sarabeth. The guests responded with whoops and applause and calls of congratulations as the bride and groom made their way down a center aisle toward the ballroom. Gina followed on the arm of Brett's best man. Rafe knew it was ridiculous to be jealous. They were simply fulfilling their roles in the wedding. But he couldn't help himself.

Ross, Charlotte, Asher and Lani fell in behind, and the rest of the guests rose and began to move in a swell from the ceremony to the hall.

Rafe lingered. He knew Gina would have official duties, photographs first, then dining at the head table, maybe making a toast. He planned to wander up to the cocktail bar on the top deck where it was a little quieter and wait his way through the next hour or so. He'd join his brothers for dinner, which he was sure would be off-the-charts delicious, but all he really wanted was to dance with Gina.

As expected, a sensational staff served a cheese-and-candied-nuts starter, followed by a crisp melon salad, a seafood cocktail, and grilled wild salmon with mushroom risotto and baby vegetables, all followed by a tray of delicate mini chocolate truffles with gold filigree. Everything was accompanied by the perfect wine pairings.

Finally, the guests migrated to the lower deck, and it was time for the first dance. A grinning Brett led Sarabeth onto the dance floor. She was radiant and clearly waltzing on air. Rafe couldn't help but smile at their obvious happiness and the oohs and aahs of the watchers.

Gina joined in then in the best man's arms. Rafe gritted his teeth, but it was only for the obligatory dance, and partway through other couples took to the floor. He made his move then, easing his way to the edge of the dance floor, successfully timing his arrival to when the song changed and Gina separated from her partner.

She looked up, seeming surprised to see him so close.

"Dance?" he drawled.

"Where have you been?" she asked as she moved into his arms.

The song the band started was thankfully slow, and he drew her close. "Waiting for you."

"I was looking for you at dinner. I was afraid you might have left."

He was surprised to hear her say that. "Never. You look stunning, you know." He chuckled. "You have a mirror, so I guess you know."

"You like the dress?" she asked.

"I like you in it."

She drew back and pouted a little.

"And I like the dress."

"I had to try on about thirty of them."

"You made a great choice. Sarabeth looks very happy."

Gina turned to look at her mother. "She is. She so deserves it. They both do."

Rafe tucked Gina's head into the crook of his shoulder, lightly feathering his fingers where her upper back was left bare by the strapless dress. "I missed you," he whispered.

"I missed you, too," she said. "It's been a busy week…"

"I'm glad it's over." He didn't know what came next for them, but he desperately wanted it to be *something*.

"Tonight may go on for a while," she warned.

"That's okay. You're free now. That's all I care about."

She tipped back her head and smiled. "I have to help with the cake-cutting later."

"I suppose I can give you up for that long." He put on a mock earnest expression. "I mean, I hear tell it's a really great cake."

She laughed and bopped him in the arm at the same time.

"Vanilla lemon curd with white chocolate buttercream," he said.

"You remembered."

"I remember everything you say to me, Gina. Everything."

The song ended and Ross appeared at Rafe's elbow. "Gina?" he asked, offering his hand.

Rafe's grip subconsciously tightened, but he knew she could hardly say no to her brother.

He forced himself to let her go and stepped back.

Ross shot him a challenging look that might have made another man back off. But there was no way Rafe was backing off from Gina. Not a chance in hell.

He moved out of the way, but only temporarily, standing a little way back from the dance floor, as Ross and Gina seemed to have a fairly intense conversation.

Lorenzo appeared at his side and handed him a drink that looked like bourbon. "How's it going?"

"Great." Rafe didn't even try to camouflage the frustration in his tone as he tossed the drink back.

His brother nodded in Gina's direction. "It's not just business between you two, is it?"

"It's not just business," Rafe admitted.

"So, what's going on?"

"I don't know." That was the truth.

"Are you sleeping with her?"

"Yes." Rafe was through keeping his feelings for Gina a secret.

"Does her brother know that?"

"Nope."

"Think he's guessed by the way you look at her?"

"Maybe." Rafe had to admit it was a possibility.

"Never thought I'd see that day." There was a thread of humor in Lorenzo's voice.

"What day is that?"

"A romance between our two families."

"You think they're too good for us?" Rafe asked a question that had been in the back of his mind since that first night with Gina.

"No. I think we're too good for them." Lorenzo gave Rafe a clap on the back. "Be careful around her."

Valencia arrived next to Lorenzo. "Honey?"

Lorenzo immediately wrapped his arm around her waist. His tone went soft. "You want to dance?"

She smiled and nodded.

Rafe took Lorenzo's empty glass to free him up for the dance floor, then deposited both glasses on a nearby tray. As the band switched songs again, Rafe looked for Gina, only to discover she was dancing with Asher. He settled back to cool his heels, swooping in again just as soon as the song ended.

It was a relief to have her back. He didn't talk, didn't

ask about either of her brothers, not wanting to break the sensual spell of being in each other's arms.

The song ended. He was determined not to give her up again. But the MC stepped up to the microphone, and with a flourish he announced the throwing of the bridal bouquet. Claps and cheers came up, and the crowd parted on the dance floor, making space for the single women.

Rafe had no choice but to step to the side with Gina as a cluster of mostly young women moved into the center of the hall, chatting and laughing at the time-honored tradition. Someone came by and grabbed Gina's hand. She resisted, but another young woman stopped as well, coaxing her to the join the growing crowd.

Rafe backed off to stay out of the way, watching Gina take a position at a far corner of the group. The drummer gave a dramatic roll on his snare drum. Turning her back to the ladies, Sarabeth laughed. Then she tossed the bouquet high in the air.

As it arced in slow motion, Gina's eyes went wide. She took a step back, almost as if she was trying to get out of the way. But the bouquet landed square in her chest and she seemed to reflexively trap it with her hands.

Rafe couldn't help but smile at her look of bewilderment.

A figure loomed up beside him—*Ross.*

"It took me a while," Ross said as the women clustered around Gina oohing and aahing and congratulating her.

She still looked disconcerted.

Rafe wasn't going to take the bait. He stayed silent, letting Ross say whatever it was he was here to say.

"To work out why you wouldn't take the money," Ross said.

"Didn't need it," Rafe responded.

"That's a lie."

Rafe shrugged. "Think whatever you like."

"I am. I do. Why take the scraps when you can latch onto the mother lode?"

Rafe turned to Ross, his eyes narrowing. "Is that supposed to be some kind of a joke?"

Ross nodded to Gina. "You've cleverly wormed your way into her life. She even caught the bouquet. You must think it's going to be smooth sailing to the altar." Ross's scowl deepened. "It won't be smooth. I'll make sure of that."

"Back *the hell* off," Rafe ground out. He couldn't believe Ross would accuse him of romancing Gina for her money.

"Sucks to get caught."

"Leave," Rafe said. "Now."

A smug expression on his face, Ross strode away.

"The family's been through a lot." It was Asher's voice on Rafe's other side.

He twisted his neck, shocked and annoyed to see Gina's other brother eyeing him up with the same suspicion.

"*She's* been through a lot," Asher continued. "You might want to keep that in mind when you're messing with her trust."

"I'm not—" Rafe started to defend himself but clamped his jaw instead. He could protest until he was blue in the face and the Edmond brothers would never listen. They thought they had him pegged.

Rafe glanced around the room, wondering what judgmental thoughts were behind the other smiling faces of the who's who of Royal.

His gaze came to Gina, and he felt a little better. The cluster of women around her had trickled to three, none that he recognized, so he started her way.

"You never know," one of the women said to her.

"Your turn next," another said.

"No, really, there's nobody, nobody at all," Gina responded.

"Tradition is tradition."

"That's superstition," Gina countered, then she saw Rafe standing close and guilt flashed across her face.

It didn't take a rocket scientist to conclude that he was the nobody. His chest suddenly felt like lead.

The women spotted him. "Ah, here's a likely candidate now," one of them sang out.

Gina's face flushed a little, and she stammered as she spoke. "He's...that's...just...Rafe."

"Business associate," Rafe offered to the curious women. He tried to give Gina a smile, but he couldn't quite pull it off. "Nice catch." His voice came out cold. "See you later." He turned away.

"Rafe!" she called behind him.

He didn't turn back, sped up instead, efficiently crossing the big room as the crowd closed behind him. Then he came out on the deck and headed straight for the closest gangplank, getting off the yacht to make his way down the dock.

He couldn't believe he'd been so blind. He and Gina were good together, sure. But it was a lark for her, a temporary, fun fling that wasn't leading anywhere near where he'd wanted it to go.

He might have had an epiphany watching her walk down that staircase with a bouquet in her hands, but that was his take, not hers. At best, she was skipping blithely through their relationship with no thought to the future. At worst, she thought the same thing as her brothers—that he had an interest in her wealth.

It was only a few blocks to the hotel, but he didn't want to go back there. Rafe didn't particularly want to *be* anywhere right now. He shucked his jacket and undid his tie, turning from the parking lot to the boardwalk and the yellow lights spilling out from the row of tourist shops and cafés.

Gina had rushed after Rafe, regretting her words and hating the way they had sounded. She'd made it sound like he was nothing special, that he wasn't the most amazing man in the world and that she wouldn't leap at an offer to spend the rest of her life with him.

Catching the bouquet had rocked her to her toes. As a young girl, she'd dreamed of catching the bouquet, of the big white wedding that was sure to follow. She'd fantasized of dressing up like a fairy princess and gliding down the aisle of a huge cathedral to meet her waiting groom. In her dreams, the groom had been faceless, a tall, dark man in a fine tux who would whisk her away on a fairy tale.

But the groom had a face now. It was *Rafe*. And it was the rest of the fantasy that had fallen away. She didn't care about the gorgeous dress, the flowers or the five-tiered cake. She didn't care about the crowds of people in the pews wishing them well or about jetting off on a fabulous honeymoon. She wanted Rafe, only Rafe, but she had no idea if he felt the same way.

Gina had been embarrassed by the inference that he might be her future groom, worried he'd feel pushed and prodded into something he wasn't anywhere near ready to even think about. She'd been so worried that he'd be uncomfortable that she'd stumbled all over herself, protesting far too much.

And now he was gone, obviously gone since she'd checked the entire ship and couldn't find a single sign of him. Even his brothers didn't know where he was.

"Gina." Sarabeth called her name from where she was standing with Brett near the bandstand.

Gina looked over and her mother motioned her forward, pointing at the cake that was being wheeled out on a tray by two waiters. The MC was getting ready to announce the cake-cutting.

"No," Gina whispered to herself. It would take forever to help hand out cake to all these guests, and she needed to find Rafe.

Her mother motioned her again, looking puzzled by Gina's lack of response.

With a last look around, she started forward as the MC made the pronouncement and the photographer got into position. She told herself this was her last official act of the night. Next, Sarabeth and Brett would wave goodbye to their guests and leave by private jet on their honeymoon to the Florida Keys.

Still glancing around for Rafe, Gina stood back while the official ceremonial cut was made. Then she moved in and smiled for some pictures. At Sarabeth's insistence, Ross moved into the frame, then Asher as well, followed by their fianceés. Gina felt like the photos would never end.

But finally, the waiters stepped in to help cut and set out the cake. While the bride and groom circulated through the guests, Gina handed out slice after slice, thanking person after person for coming to the wedding. The cake lineup finally ended with a good portion of the huge cake remaining.

After it was wheeled back to the kitchen, the MC announced the wedding couple was taking their leave from the main gangway. Everyone was invited to gather there and bid them farewell.

Gina hugged her mother and her new stepfather goodbye. The crowd cheered and waved them across the gangplank and into a waiting limousine that drove them off on their honeymoon. Many of the guests chose the moment to leave the party as well, crossing the gangplank in couples and groups, heading into their cars in the sprawling parking lot.

Gina moved to one side to keep herself out of the way, finding Ross and Charlotte with their son, Ben, balanced on her hip standing along the rail. "Have you seen Rafe?" she asked them.

"No," Ross answered. "Why?"

She didn't want to talk about the bridal bouquet debacle, or her fear that Rafe left the wedding reception hurt and angry. She settled on something straightforward. "He was my escort."

"I can get you whatever you need," Ross said.

"No, it's not that—"

A figure suddenly loomed up in front of them, and Gina was stunned to recognize Billy Holmes. He was dressed like a guest in an impeccable suit, and she wondered just when he'd infiltrated the crowd. His black hair was unruly. His lips were drawn in a thin line. And there was an unmistakable glitter of hatred in his pale green eyes.

"Well, well, well," he drawled. "My beloved sister and brother."

Ross quickly urged Charlotte and Ben to leave and go back inside. But when he tried to do the same with Gina, Billy stopped him.

"Not so fast," he said, menace in his tone.

Gina stilled, afraid of what Billy might do, wondering if he had become desperate. People were still streaming off the main gangplank. The party was breaking up, and Billy had obviously timed his appearance.

"You shouldn't be here," Ross growled in an undertone, shifting closer to Gina.

"Would I miss the big day?" Billy taunted, sounding chipper but brittle. "The big family day."

Asher materialized on Gina's other side. "This isn't your family, Billy."

Gina could sense the coiled tension in each of her two brothers. She knew they were sizing the other man up, deciding what they could do to subdue him.

"You sure got that right," Billy barked back. "It *should* have been my family. By blood this is my family." He raised his voice to the crowd. "Wedding's over! Everyone off the ship. Only Edmonds allowed now. This—" he stared pointedly at Ross and then Gina, then Asher "—is a family matter."

The guests looked over, some confused, some concerned. Mostly, they hurried more quickly over the gangplank.

As the crowd thinned to nothing, Ross and Asher

shared a look. Their expressions said they were going to make a move against Billy.

"Uh-uh," Billy chided, taking a step back. He patted the breast pocket of his jacket meaningfully. "You don't want to see what I'm carrying under here. I came prepared."

Gina's blood turned to ice at the thought that Billy might be armed and mean them harm. She was grateful Charlotte and Ben were safely inside; presumably, so was Lani. She hoped they stayed far away from this confrontation.

"What do you want?" Ross asked Billy.

Gina was wondering the same thing. It was a risk for him to show his face. One or more of the guests might have recognized him and called the police. His picture had been plastered all over the Texas news for months now. She desperately hoped someone would think to alert the authorities.

Another person crossed the gangplank, boarding the yacht. With the glare of the parking lot lights in her eyes, it took Gina a moment to recognize Rusty.

"Dad?" she asked in astonishment. He should have been back in Royal.

"The gang's all here," Billy said with satisfaction as Rusty halted, taking them in.

"I came," he said shortly to Billy. "Time for you to live up to your end."

"What's the hurry?" Billy asked, his voice laced with faux charm. "The party's just getting started."

"Where's the money?" Rusty asked.

"You know your big mistake?" Billy bit out. "Thinking this was about the money. It was *never* about the money."

"Then why'd you steal it?" Ross demanded.

"To hit you where it *hurts*!"

"In our bank account," Asher said.

It didn't make a whole lot of sense, since the Edmonds had plenty of money left.

"No," Billy barked, taking a couple of quick paces to the side and then pacing back again.

Gina glanced around the deck and saw nobody else was left.

"You Edmonds," Billy continued. "Always bigger than life, swaggering around town, looking down on the peasants."

"Peasants?" Gina asked, baffled by the description.

"Give back the money," Rusty said. "Like you promised. Return it all, and we can talk. We can approach the DA, work out a deal, make things right."

"Simple as that?" Billy asked sarcastically.

"It can be. No guarantees."

"You wouldn't press charges?"

"No," Rusty said.

"Why, pray tell, *not*?" Billy looked even angrier with Rusty now, and Gina couldn't stop thinking about the gun he claimed to have in his pocket.

"You know why not," her dad said quietly.

"Because I'm your son." There was a sharp challenge in Billy's voice.

"That's right," Rusty said.

Everyone, including Billy, looked shocked by the admission.

"It's all there," Rusty continued, sizing Billy up. "In your eyes, your voice, your determination and drive. You're more like me than any of the rest."

Gina, Ross and Asher all stared at their father in open astonishment.

"Dad?" Ross asked.

"Don't you dare interrupt!" Billy's anger swung to Ross. "He's talking to me now, *me*, not you. You had *everything*. Russell Jr., the namesake, the eldest, the golden child. The heir apparent who got everything while I got nothing." Billy glared at Asher. "Not even the family name. *You* got the family name, Asher. You just showed up with your mother, and Rusty took you right under his wing. You got the family name, the company, the money, the prestige and power. What did I get?" Billy's anger seemed to increase by the minute.

"You're not returning the money, are you?" Rusty took Billy's attention back on himself.

"To save your hide?" he sneered. "To save the lot of you the pain and humiliation of being the town pariahs?"

"To save yourself a long jail sentence," Ross said.

"It didn't have to *be* like this." Billy squeezed his eyes shut for a moment, sounding more and more unhinged. "I thought you'd take me in, give me my fair turn, treat me the way you treated your precious Ross, that upstart Asher, and your flawless princess Gina all those years while I was scrambling for pennies."

Ross jumped in. "You have no idea what you're talking about."

"Don't I?" Billy challenged.

"He *disowned* me," Ross pointed out.

Billy leaned toward Ross. "Welcome to the club."

"He didn't even know about you."

Billy didn't seem to hear Ross's response. Instead, he gave a cold chuckle. "Taste of your own medicine, huh?

You should know that was me." He mimicked the sound of an explosion, dramatically spreading his fingers and pulling his hands apart. "Charlotte was like a grenade with the pin pulled. That was a masterstroke, that was."

"You sent Charlotte back to hurt Ross?" Gina's fear was being replaced by anger now. "What is *wrong* with you?"

"But it was Dad who tried to drive us apart," Ross said.

"I thought I'd have to work a lot harder," Billy admitted, still sporting a chilling smile. "But you Edmonds were a domino line of dysfunction just waiting to fall."

"*I* went to *jail* over this," Asher said, his voice laced with anger.

"All part of the plot," Billy stated with satisfaction. "Frame the interloper. Alienate the golden child."

"I underestimated you," Rusty told him.

"Damn straight you underestimated me."

Rusty spoke again. "I was wrong, and I'm sorry."

Gina had never in her life heard her father utter those words. It was beyond jarring that he'd used them with Billy of all people.

"You're my son, Billy, my flesh and blood. You're smart, driven, tenacious." Rusty looked oddly proud of him. "I should have acknowledged you, welcomed you into the heart of our family."

"The *heart*?" Gina asked with incredulity. If they were coming clean here, then she was coming clean, too.

The tone of her voice got everyone's attention.

"There was no heart!" she cried out. "Like Billy just said, we're a row of dysfunctional dominoes waiting to fall." She pointed to her chest. "I'm a grown woman, an educated, intelligent woman. But I'm treated like a decoration, pampered with possessions but discounted, ignored, never given a chance to do anything or to be anyone. My world revolves around the male Edmond whims, smiling at business functions, chatting up company associates. Nobody ever asked me what I could contribute."

Rusty's jaw dropped slightly.

"I was bullied and undermined at every turn," Ross said to Rusty. "You belittled me. You hurt the woman I loved. Then you threw me away when I didn't fit your mold."

Rusty jerked back, staring at them as if he'd been hit.

"You sat back and *let* them frame me," Asher told him. "You had so little faith in me that you assumed I was a criminal on circumstantial evidence. You think Billy's like you? *Yeah*, Billy's like you. The rest of us are *not*."

Rusty stared straight ahead for a moment, a haunted expression in his eyes. "I deserved that."

"You're a conniving man," Ross said, clearly not finished yet. "In big ways and small, you schemed to make us what you wanted no matter what it did to our own lives."

There was a long silence after that.

"I'm sorry to you all," Rusty finally murmured, his voice so low and husky that Gina thought she'd misheard.

"I'm sorry," he said more firmly. "You're my children. You're all I have, and I'm going to do better. And Billy—"

Rusty turned, and Gina looked to where Billy had been standing just moments ago.

The deck was empty, and they all stared in stupefied silence until an engine revved loudly in the parking lot below. A pair of tires screeched and a black sports car zigzagged toward the exit. It was obvious Billy was making a run for it.

"I don't get it," Gina said as the car sped away. "What did he want?"

"Acknowledgment?" Ross speculated. "Maybe he thinks he got it?"

"More like he knew he'd go to jail if he stayed," Asher noted.

"He's family," Rusty said.

"You're saying you'd *help* him get out of this?" Ross asked incredulously.

"I'd at least get him a good lawyer."

"I don't think he's returning the money," Gina observed, looking at the now-empty road.

"I hope it's brought him some peace," Rusty said sadly.

"He stole *millions of dollars*," Asher reminded him.

"He wanted to be part of the family."

"He went about it in the worst way possible." Gina looked at her brothers and her father then, wondering what happened next.

Was Rusty's apology to them a first step? Could they pull it together and salvage their family?

"We will," Rusty seemed to understand her unspoken question. "This is my doing. It's mine to fix, and I'm *going* to fix it."

Gina immediately thought of Rafe. The rift with Rafe was hers to fix, and she was determined to make amends. He might not love her, but she was head over heels for him. She was going to make that clear as soon as she got back to Royal.

She was laying her cards on the table. The two of them didn't have a business relationship. This wasn't a fling or friends with benefits or any temporary euphemism someone wanted to give it.

Gina wanted a *real* relationship. She wanted to be Rafe's significant other, the woman he spent his downtime with, plus family dinners, barbecues, everything other couples did together and more...

"I'm exhausted," she said to her father and brothers, feeling impatient to get going. "I'm getting my things and heading home."

Gina made her way toward the stern of the yacht where a little staircase would take her back to the captain's cabin for her purse.

"Gina?" Rafe's voice startled her as he stepped from the shadows.

She couldn't believe it was him silhouetted against the deck lights. "Rafe?" But he was here, and her heart sang with joy.

"Hi," he said, a hesitant expression on his face.

She took a step closer. "I'm so sorry."

"It's okay."

"It's not."

He canted his head back along the deck. "I overheard just now."

"Billy?" she asked in surprise.

"I stuck close in case he tried something stupid."

She shuddered. "I thought he had a gun."

"He might have had a gun. He's pretty desperate."

"I know." Her knees suddenly felt weak in reaction.

Rafe seemed to sense it and stepped forward, reaching out to her.

She gripped his forearms for support.

"I knew you struggled with your father," he said, searching her expression. "But I had no idea of all that you'd been through."

"It's not going to continue," she told him.

"It seemed like you cleared the air."

"I have ideas, and I'm pushing them forward."

"Good for you." His smile seemed sad, and she remembered how they'd left things after the bouquet toss.

Her shoulders drooped. "Back there. Inside, I mean. I…I didn't mean for you to think…"

Rafe shifted closer. "Think what?"

"That you were nobody to me. That you were a business associate or a friend or something run-of-the-mill like that."

"Ross and Asher think I'm after your money."

The statement shocked her to silence.

"You know I'm not after your money, right?" Rafe asked, an earnest expression in his eyes.

She was baffled by the question. "I keep trying to give you my money, and you keep turning it down."

He chuckled in what seemed like relief.

"And the chamber fund," she continued. "That was a *lot* of money you turned down."

"I don't want your money."

"I know."

"I won't take it."

"Okay." She didn't know why he was pressing the point.

"You should write up an iron-clad prenup so you and

your brothers, your father, and anyone else who cares will know that I am definitely not after a single penny of Edmond money."

Gina's mind stuck on the word *prenup*. She swallowed. "A *what*?"

He eased her closer and smoothed her hair. "When I walked away from you, I was hurt and angry. But then I got lonely, and then I got *scared*. Scared that I'd never see you again, never hold you again, never make love with you again. After that, I got determined."

Was he working his way up to the part about a prenup? She couldn't tell. "Rafe, what are you saying?"

"I'm saying that I'm determined to stay with you forever. I love you, Gina. And I hope you love me back, because I don't ever want to feel that kind of loneliness again."

Joy rushed through her, making her sway with relief. "I love you," she whispered through her clogged throat.

Rafe instantly wrapped his arms around her, holding her flush against his strength.

"There's not a lot open on the boardwalk this time of night," he whispered in her ear. "But I did manage to find this."

He reached into his pocket and produced a little box.

Gina drew back to look, her heart skipping a beat as he opened the box to reveal a stylized platinum band inset with a small sapphire, an emerald and a diamond.

"We can get something nicer," he said. "Design whatever we want. But I was in a hurry to seal the deal."

"It's beautiful," she whispered. She absolutely loved it.

"Will you marry me, Gina?"

"Yes." She nodded, her eyes going misty. "Yes! I love you, Rafe. I love you so much."

Epilogue

Gina's wedding was a far cry from her mother's yacht-board gala and completely different from the frothy extravaganzas she'd imagined as a little girl.

Her decoration was the fall foliage, bright on the trees at the Cortez-Williams Ranch. The air was comfortably cool midafternoon. The guests seated on folding chairs in the backyard were family and close friends, many long-standing members of the TCC.

She waited with her father on the back porch of the ranch house while bridesmaids Valencia and Anastasia walked over the cobblestoned pool deck toward the makeshift aisle. Rusty was all smiles dressed in his finest tux. His shave was close, his hair neatly trimmed as music from Diego's scaled-down acoustic band wafted on the breeze.

Rusty looked more at peace than Gina had ever seen him.

"Did you get hold of Antoinette?" she asked him.

"We don't need to talk about her right now." He took another look at Gina's breezy white cocktail-length wedding dress.

It was flat lace, a V-neck with spaghetti straps, a wide waistband and a full skirt that fluttered over her knees. Her bouquet was a ribbon-tied bunch of wild-flowers picked just this morning on the ranch. She wore little white flats on her feet, great for walking on the lush lawn, while her hair was a casual low ponytail with a few waves and twists, just loose enough to frame her face.

"I'm curious," Gina said. "What did she say? How did she react?"

"We had a long talk, and she accepted my apology."

Gina knew he would be relieved. "So that's every-one?"

After the blowout with Billy, Rusty had become de-termined to turn over a new leaf with his immediate family and also to make amends with his ex-wives and lovers, along with some other folks he'd wronged in the past.

"That's everyone. And this is your wedding. Today is all about you."

"All about me?"

"Yes."

"Then can we talk about the methane energy pro-posal?" she asked, judging that she had about one minute left before Anastasia arrived at the greenery-decorated archway and the music changed for the bridal procession.

"No. I only have one daughter, and she's only having one wedding, and we're *not* talking business."

"You can't say no to the bride, Dad."

"That's why we're not talking business today."

"Did you read the report?"

The music changed, and everyone rose from their chairs.

"It's time," he said.

"Did you read the report?"

"Yes, I read it." He tucked her hand into his elbow. "Walking, Gina. We're walking. You don't want Rafe to think you're having second thoughts."

She started to walk along the pool deck. "I'm not having second thoughts."

"I know. Rafe's a good man."

"He made me write a prenup."

"I know that, too. He showed it to me. He was crystal clear on not taking any Edmond money."

"He signed it. I didn't. I'm not going to."

Rusty smiled as they rounded the pool. "You are the chattiest bride in the world."

"Known a lot of brides, have you?" she asked slyly.

Rafe came into view then, and she met his eyes, drinking in the depths of his dark gaze, watching his lips curve into a bright smile. His love seemed to reach out the length of the lawn, and she sent hers back to meet it.

Rusty squeezed her hand as they walked between the two rows of their close family and friends.

Gina smiled for everyone, but her focus was on Rafe, the man she loved, the man who was about to become her husband for better or worse, forever and ever.

She made it to the archway where Rafe stood with Lorenzo and Matias.

Rusty gave her a hug and a quick kiss on the cheek, and then her groom took her hand.

She passed her bouquet to Valencia to take Rafe's other hand for the ceremony.

Their vows flew by quickly, and soon they were exchanging rings. Then the preacher was pronouncing them husband and wife, and Rafe lifted her off the ground for a long, smoldering kiss.

The guests cheered and tossed flower pedals, and they were immediately surrounded by well-wishers.

Charlotte and JJ had joined in with Rafe's parents to produce a backyard barbecue feast. Mrs. Yeoh had baked an amazing honey orange wedding cake with spicy chocolate ganache.

Matias's band set up their speakers, and the dinner quickly turned into a rollicking dance.

When Gina finally sat down for a rest, Lila handed her a glass of refreshing iced tea and joined her at the table. "Did you hear the good news?"

"That Rafe married me?" Gina joked, lifting her glass in a mock toast before taking a drink.

Lila grinned and drank along with her. "I mean they got the money back. Well, most of it, anyway. Enough that none of the Royal businesses are at risk anymore."

"And Billy?" Gina asked, so happy to hear the news.

He hadn't been seen since the night at Mustang Point when his sports car slid off the road and into deep water during his escape.

"No sign of him. Could be sharks, or he could be on a beach in the Maldives."

"I hope he's on a beach." Gina couldn't bring herself to wish him any ill, especially now that they had the money back, and especially understanding that he'd been yet another victim of her father's misadventures. Her gaze shifted to Rusty where he was down on the grass, tux and all, playing with his grandson, Ben.

"Lani says someone sent Antoinette a million dollars," Lila confided.

"You think it was Billy?" Gina asked. It was oddly encouraging to think a man like Billy might finally be taking care of his mother after all this.

"Or it could be Rusty," Lila said.

"Possibly." Gina watched her father a minute longer, thinking it was like getting to know a whole new person.

Valencia plunked down on a chair next to Gina, her feet bare against the grass, her sandals dangling from one hand. "You and Rafe thinking about babies?" she asked.

The question took Gina by surprise. "We haven't even finished the wedding cake."

"I see you looking."

"At?"

"Ben. Adorable little guy, isn't he?"

"He is," Gina agreed. "But I was looking at Rusty, thinking how much he'd changed."

"Oh." Valencia seemed disappointed.

Gina took in her expression. "Wait. Why are you asking…?"

Valencia grinned and touched her hand to her stomach.

"No way!" Gina laughed, delighted with the news. "Tito and Tita are going to be thrilled!" Gina knew Rafe's parents would adore some grandchildren, the more the better as far as they were concerned.

"Lorenzo can't wait to tell them."

"Is it still a secret?" Gina whispered.

A grinning Lila squeezed Valencia on the shoulder. "That's fantastic!"

"We wanted to wait until after your wedding. But now we'll start telling people. You should think about it."

"Maybe," Gina said. "Not tonight, though."

"Well, *I'll* keep you company," Lila said.

Both Gina and Valencia swung their heads her way.

"You *are*?" Valencia asked.

"Mine *is* a secret," Lila said. "It's really early. I just told Zach a couple of days ago."

Gina and Valencia both mimed zipping their lips and tossing away the key.

Rafe strode their way, his gaze drinking in Gina as he approached. "What are you all talking about?"

"Babies," Valencia said.

He reached for Gina's hand and drew her to her feet, wrapping an arm around her waist and giving her a quick kiss on the lips. "I'm in." He looked at his watch. "Can we do it now?"

"I like your attitude," Valencia said on a laugh.

Lorenzo joined them then, along with Zach.

"Rafe wants to make a baby on their honeymoon," Valencia told Lorenzo.

His eyes lit up. "Did you tell them?"

She nodded.

"Tell them what?" Rafe asked.

"Not Rafe, just the gals."

"Better congratulate me, little brother. It might be your wedding, but I'm going to be a daddy next summer."

"No way." Rafe grinned in delight and gave Lorenzo a hug.

Zach cleared his throat, and everyone looked his way. "Not to be outdone, Lorenzo." He pointed to Lila's stomach. "You're not the only one increasing the TCC junior membership next year."

"Congratulations, Lila." Lorenzo reached out his arms to give her a hug.

"I sense a challenge," Rafe said.

Gina held up her palms to slow things down, laughing at the same time. "We need to talk about this."

"Oh, don't you worry, Princess," Rafe rumbled in her ear, pulling her closer. "We most definitely will."

* * * * *

*Look for the first book in the next
Texas Cattleman's Club series,
Fathers and Sons, available next month!*

An Heir of His Own

by USA TODAY *bestselling author
Janice Maynard*

#2833 AN HEIR OF HIS OWN
Texas Cattleman's Club: Fathers and Sons
by Janice Maynard

When Cammie Wentworth finds an abandoned baby, the only man who can help is her ex, entrepreneur Drake Rhodes. Drake isn't looking to play family, but as the sparks burn hotter, will these two find their second chance?

#2834 WAYS TO WIN AN EX
Dynasties: The Carey Center • by Maureen Child

Serena Carey once wanted forever with hotelier Jack Colton, but he left her brokenhearted. Now he's back, and she, reluctantly, needs his help on an event that could make her future—she just has to resist the chemistry that still sizzles between them...

#2835 JUST FOR THE HOLIDAYS...
Sambrano Studios • by Adriana Herrera

The last man casting director Perla Sambrano wants to see is Gael Montez. But the handsome A-lister is perfect for her new show. When they're snowed in during a script reading, will he become the leading man in her heart just in time for Christmas?

#2836 THE STAKES OF FAKING IT
Brooklyn Nights • by Joanne Rock

The daughter of a conman, actress Tana Blackstone has put her family's past and the people they hurt, like Chase Serrano, behind her. But when Chase needs a fake fiancée, she can't refuse. Soon, this fake relationship reveals very real temptation...

#2837 STRICTLY CONFIDENTIAL
The Grants of DC • by Donna Hill

With her family's investments in jeopardy, Lexi Randall needs the help of real estate developer Montgomery Grant, who just happens to also be a notorious playboy. When the professional turns *very* personal, can she still save the family business—and her heart?

#2838 SECRETS, VEGAS STYLE
by Kira Sinclair

Cultivating his bad-boy reputation, nightclub CEO Dominic Mercado uses it to help those in need and keep away heartbreak. But when his best friend's sister, Meredith Forrester, who's always been off-limits, gets too close, their undeniable attraction may risk everything...

---

*The last man casting director Perla Sambrano wants
to see is Gael Montez. But the handsome A-lister is
perfect for her new show. Now, snowed in during a
script reading, will he become the leading man in
her heart just in time for Christmas?*

Read on for a sneak peek at
Just for the Holidays…
by Adriana Herrera.

"Sure, why don't you tell me how to feel, Gael, that's always
been a special skill of yours." She knew that was not the
way they would arrive at civility, but she was tired of his
sulking.

She could see his jaw working and a flush of pink
working up his throat. She should leave this alone. This
could not lead anywhere good. She'd already felt what his
touch did to her. Already confirmed that the years and the
distance had done nothing to temper her feelings for him,
and here she was provoking him. Goading an answer out
of him that would wreck her no matter what it was. And he
would tell her because Gael had never been a coward. And
he'd already called her bluff once today.

He moved fast and soon she was pressed to a wall or a
door, she didn't really care, because all of her concentration
was going toward Gael's hands on her. His massive, rock-
hard body pressed to her, and she wished, really wished, she
had the strength to resist him. But all she did was hold on
tighter when he pressed his hot mouth to her ear.

"I've told myself a thousand times today that I'm not supposed to want you as much as I do." He sounded furious, and if she hadn't known him as well as she did, she would've missed the regret lacing his words. He gripped her to him, and desire shot up inside her like Fourth of July fireworks, from her toes and exploding inside her chest.

"Wouldn't it be something if we could make ourselves want the things that we can have," she said bitterly. He scoffed at that, and she didn't know if it was in agreement or denial of what she'd said. It was impossible to focus with his hands roaming over her like they were.

"I don't want to talk about it." *It. I* and *T.* She had no idea what the *it* even was. It could've been so many things. His father's abandonment, their love story that had been laid to waste. The years they had lost, everything they could never get back. Two letters to encompass so much loss and heartbreak. It was on the tip of her tongue to demand answers, to push him to stop hiding, to tell her the truth for once. But she could not make herself speak, the pain in his eyes stealing her ability to do so.

He ran a hand over his head, like he didn't know where to start. Like the moment was too much for him, and for a moment she thought he would actually walk away, leave her standing there. He kissed her instead.

Don't miss what happens next in…
Just for the Holidays…
by Adriana Herrera,
the next book in her new Sambrano Studios series!

Available November 2021 wherever
Harlequin Desire books and ebooks are sold.

Harlequin.com

HDEXP1021